As they passed through into the wide swee saw the wind picking up, swirling little spirals of sand, twisting them up into the sky. Kareef felt the same way every time he looked at her. Tangled up in her.

He felt her dark head nestle on his shoulder. Looking down at her in surprise, he saw her eyes were closed. She was sleeping against him. His gaze roamed her face.

God, he wanted to kiss her.

More than kiss. He wanted to strip her naked and feast on every inch of her supple flesh. He wanted to explore the mountains of her breasts and the valley between. The low, flat plain of her belly and the hot citadel between her thighs. He wanted to devour her like a conqueror seizing an ancient land for his own use, beneath his hands, beneath his control.

But the old days were over.

He was King of Qusay, yet unable to have the one thing he most desired. No strength could take her. No brutality could force her. He couldn't act on his desire. Not at the expense of her happiness.

Many years ago there were two Mediterranean islands, ruled as one kingdom—Adamas. But bitter family feuds ripped Adamas apart and the islands went their separate ways. The Greek Karedes family reigned supreme over glamorous Aristo, and the smouldering Al'Farisi sheikhs commanded the desert lands of Calista!

When the Aristan king died, an illegitimate daughter was discovered—Stefania, the rightful heir to the throne! Ruthlessly, the Calistan Sheikh King Zakari seduced her into marriage, to claim absolute power, but was over-awed by her purity—and succumbed to love. Now they rule both Aristo and Calista together, in the spirit of hope and prosperity.

But a black mark hangs over the Calistan royal family still. As young boys, three of King Zakari's brothers were kidnapped for ransom by pirates. Two returned safely, but the youngest was swept out to sea and never found—presumed dead. Then, at Stefania's coronation, a stranger appeared in their midst— the ruler of a nearby kingdom, Qusay. A stranger with scars on his wrists from pirates' ropes. A stranger who knows nothing of his past—only his future as a king!

What will happen when Xavian, King of Qusay, discovers that he's living the wrong life?

And who will claim the Qusay throne if the truth is unveiled?

**Find out more in the exciting,
brand-new Modern Romance™ mini-series**

DARK-HEARTED DESERT MEN
*A kingdom torn apart by scandal; a throne left empty;
four smouldering desert princes…Which one will
claim the crown—and who will they claim as their brides?*

Book 1. WEDLOCKED: BANISHED SHEIKH,
UNTOUCHED QUEEN
by Carol Marinelli
Book 2. TAMED: THE BARBARIAN KING
by Jennie Lucas
Book 3. FORBIDDEN: THE SHEIKH'S VIRGIN
by Trish Morey
Book 4. SCANDAL: HIS MAJESTY'S LOVE-CHILD
by Annie West

TAMED: THE BARBARIAN KING

BY
JENNIE LUCAS

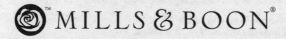

MILLS & BOON

First published in Great Britain 2010
Harlequin Mills & Boon Limited,
Eton House, 18-24 Paradise Road, Richmond, Surrey TW9 1SR

Tamed: The Barbarian King
© Harlequin Books S.A. 2010

Special thanks and acknowledgement are given to Jennie Lucas for her contribution to the *Dark-Hearted Desert Men* series

ISBN: 978 0 263 87788 5

Harlequin Mills & Boon policy is to use papers that are natural, renewable and recyclable products and made from wood grown in sustainable forests. The logging and manufacturing process conform to the legal environmental regulations of the country of origin.

Printed and bound in Spain
by Litografia Rosés, S.A., Barcelona

Jennie Lucas grew up dreaming about faraway lands. At fifteen, hungry for experience beyond the borders of her small Idaho city, she went to a Connecticut boarding school on scholarship. She took her first solo trip to Europe at sixteen, then put off college and travelled around the US, supporting herself with jobs as diverse as gas station cashier and newspaper advertising assistant.

At twenty-two she met the man who would be her husband. After their marriage, she graduated from Kent State with a degree in English. Seven years after she started writing, she got the magical call from London that turned her into a published author.

Since then life has been hectic, with a new writing career, a sexy husband and two babies under two, but she's having a wonderful (albeit sleepless) time. She loves immersing herself in dramatic, glamorous, passionate stories. Maybe she can't physically travel to Morocco or Spain right now, but for a few hours a day, while her children are sleeping, she can be there in her books.

Jennie loves to hear from her readers. You can visit her website at www.jennielucas.com, or drop her a note at jennie@jennielucas.com

To my fellow authors of the *Dark-Hearted Desert Men* series: Carol Marinelli, Trish Morey and Annie West. You girls rock!

Plus an extra heap of thanks to Trish Morey, who's the one who got me into all this trouble in the first place.

CHAPTER ONE

MARRYING a man she didn't love was surprisingly easy, Jasmine Kouri thought as she handed her empty champagne flute to a passing waiter. Why had she wasted so much time struggling to be alone? She should have done this a year ago.

Her engagement party was in full force. All of Qusay's high society—everyone who'd once scorned her—was now milling beneath the white pavilion on the edge of the Mediterranean Sea, sipping Cristal in solid gold flutes as they toasted her engagement to the second richest man in Qusay.

Her fiancé had spared no expense. Jasmine's fifteen-carat diamond ring scattered prisms and rainbows of refracted sunlight every time she moved her left hand. It was also very heavy, and the pale green chiffon dress he'd chosen for her in Paris felt hot as her skirts swirled in the desert wind. Across the wide grassy vista, the turrets of his sprawling Italianate mansion flew red flags emblazoned with his personal crest.

Then again, Umar Hajjar never spared any expense—on anything. Everything he owned, from his world-class racehorses to his homes around the world, proclaimed his money and prestige. He'd pursued Jasmine for a year in New York, and yesterday, she'd suddenly accepted his proposal. This party was Umar's first step in making the people of Qusay forget her old scandal. He would shape Jasmine into his perfect bride, the same as he trained a promising colt into a winner: at any cost.

But that wasn't why Jasmine's heart was pounding as she looked anxiously through the crowds in the pavilion. She didn't care about money. She was after something far more precious.

Jewel-laden socialites pressed forward to congratulate her, including some whose vicious gossip had ruined her when she was young and defenseless. But it would be bad manners to remember that now, so Jasmine just thanked them and smiled until her cheeks hurt.

Then she caught her breath as she saw the people she'd been waiting for.

Her family.

The last time she'd seen them, Jasmine had been a scared sixteen-year-old girl, packed off into poverty and exile by her harsh, heartbroken father and quietly weeping mother. Now because of this marriage, no one would ever be able hurt Jasmine—or her family—ever again.

With a joyful cry, she held her arms wide, and her grown-up sisters ran to embrace her.

"I'm proud of you, my daughter," her father said gruffly, patting her on the shoulder. "At last you've done well."

"Oh, my precious child." Her mother hugged her tearfully, kissing her cheek. "It's too long you've been away!"

Both her parents had grown older. Her proud father was stooped, her mother gray. The sisters Jasmine remembered as skinny children were now plump matrons with husbands and children of their own. As her family embraced her, the wind blew around Jasmine's ladylike dress, swirling around them all in waves of sea-foam chiffon.

It was all worth it, she thought in a rush of emotion. To be with her family again, to be back at home and have a place in the world, she would have given up a hundred careers in New York. She would have married Umar a thousand times.

"I missed you all so much," Jasmine whispered. But all too soon, she was forced to pull away from her family to greet other guests. Moments later, she felt Umar's hand on her arm.

He smiled down at her. "Happy, darling?"

"Yes," she replied, wiping away the streaks of her earlier tears. Umar hated to see her mussed. "But some of the guests are growing impatient for dinner. Who is this special guest of yours and why is he so late?"

"You'll see," he replied, leaning down to kiss her cheek. Tall and thin and in his late forties, Umar Hajjar was the type of man who wore a designer suit to his stables. His face was pale and wrinkle-free with the careful application of sunscreen; his dark gray hair was slicked back with gel. He tilted his head. "Listen."

Frowning, she listened, then gradually heard a

sound like thunder. She looked up, but as usual in the desert island kingdom, there were no clouds, just clear sky blending into sea in endless shades of blue. "What is that?"

"It's our guest." Umar's smile widened. "The king."

She sucked in her breath.

"The…king?" Sudden fear pinched her heart. "What king?"

He laughed. "There is only one king, darling."

As if in slow motion, she looked back across the wide grass.

Three men on horseback had just come through the massive wrought-iron front gate. The Hajjar security guards were bowing low, their noses almost to the ground, as the leader of the horsemen rode past, followed by two men in black robes.

They all had rifles and hard, glowering faces, but the leader was far taller and more broad-shouldered than the others. A ceremonial jeweled dagger at his hip proclaimed his status while the hard look in his blue eyes betrayed his ruthlessness. Beneath the hot Qusani sun, his robes were stark white against his deeply tanned skin as he leapt gracefully down from his black stallion.

Shaking in sudden panic, Jasmine looked at him, praying she was wrong. It couldn't be him. Couldn't!

But when she looked at his handsome, brutal face, she could not deny his identity. For thirteen years, she'd seen his face in her dreams.

Kareef Al'Ramiz, the barbarian prince of the desert.

The party guests recognized him with a low gasp that echoed her own.

Kareef. The man who'd seduced and deserted her to shame and exile. The man who'd caused the loneliness and grief of half her life. The man who'd made her pay so dearly for the crime of loving him.

And in a few days, Kareef Al'Ramiz would be crowned king of all Qusay.

Fierce hatred flashed through her, hatred so pure it nearly caused her to stagger. She clutched at Umar's arm. "What is he doing here?"

His thin lips curved in a smile. "The king is my friend. Are you impressed? It's part of my plan. Come."

He pulled her across the grass to greet the royal arrival. She tried to resist, but Umar kept dragging her forward in his thin, sinewy grip. The colors of white tent and green grass and blue sea seemed to blend and melt around her. Trying to catch her breath, to regain control, she twisted her engagement ring tightly around her finger. The enormous diamond felt hard and cold against her skin.

"Sire!" Hajjar called jovially across the lawn. "You do me great honor!"

"This had better be important, Umar," the other man growled. "Only for you would I return to the city in the middle of a ride."

At the sound of Kareef's voice—the deep, low timbre that had once sounded like music to her—the swirls of color started to spin faster. She started to fear she might faint at her own party. How would Umar react to that?

Marry me, Jasmine. Kareef's long-ago whisper echoed in her mind. He'd stroked her cheek, looking down at her with the deep hunger of desire. *Marry me.*

No! She couldn't face Kareef after all these years. Not now. *Not ever!*

Her heart pounded furiously in her chest. "I have to go," she croaked, pulling frantically away from Umar's grasp. "Excuse me—"

Startled by her strength, Umar abruptly let go. Knocked off balance, she stumbled forward and fell across the grass in an explosion of pale green chiffon.

She heard a low exclamation. Suddenly hands were on her, lifting her to her feet.

She felt the electricity of a rough touch, so masculine and strong, so different from Umar's cool, slender hands. She looked up.

Kareef's handsome, implacable face was silhouetted against the sun as he lifted her to her feet. His ruthless eyes were full of shadow. Blinding light cast a halo around his black hair against the unrelenting blue sky.

His hand was still wrapped over hers as their eyes locked. His pupils dilated.

"Jasmine," he breathed, his fingers tightening on hers.

She couldn't answer. Couldn't even breathe. She dimly heard the cry of the seagulls soaring over the nearby Mediterranean, heard the buzz of insects. She was barely aware of the two hundred highborn guests behind them, watching from the pavilion.

Time had stopped. There was only the two of them. She saw him. She felt his touch on her skin. Exactly as she'd dreamed every night for the last thirteen years, in dark unwilling dreams she'd had alone in her New York penthouse.

Umar stepped between them.

"Sire," the older man said, beaming. "Allow me to present Jasmine Kouri. My bride."

Kareef stared down at her beautiful face in shock.

He'd never thought he would see Jasmine Kouri again. Seeing her so unexpectedly—*touching* her—caused a blast of ice and fire to surge through his body, from his hair to his fingertips.

Against his will, his eyes devoured every detail of her face. Her long black eyelashes trembling against her creamy skin. The pink tip of her tongue darting out to lick the center of her full, red lips.

Jasmine's dark hair, once long and stick-straight, now was thickly layered past her shoulders, cascading over a flowy, diaphanous dress that seemed straight out of a 1930s Hollywood movie. The gown skimmed her full breasts and hips, tightly belted at her slim waist. Her graceful, slender arms could be seen through long sheer sleeves.

She was almost entirely covered from head to toe, showing bare skin only at the collarbone and hands, but the effect was devastating. She looked glamorous. *Untouchable.* He wanted to grab her shoulders, to touch and taste and feel her all over and know she was real. Just the mere contact of his fingers against hers burned his skin.

Then he realized what Umar Hajjar had said.

Jasmine—Hajjar's bride?

As if he'd been struck by a blow, Kareef abruptly released her. He glanced down at his fingers and was almost bewildered to find them whole. After the electricity he'd felt touching her hand, he'd half expected to find his fingers burned beyond recognition.

With a deep breath, he slowly looked up at her. "You—are married?"

Jasmine's dark eyes met his, stabbing into his soul as deeply as a blade. Licking her lips nervously, she didn't answer.

"Not yet," Umar purred beside her. "But we will be. Immediately following the Qais Cup."

Kareef continued to look at Jasmine, but she didn't speak. Not one word.

Once, she used to chatter away in his company— she'd cajoled away his bad moods, making him laugh in spite of himself. He'd found her easy conversation relaxing. Charming. Perhaps because it was so natural—so unguarded and real. She'd been shy at first, a bookish girl more comfortable with reading newspapers and studying charts than speaking to the son of a sheikh. But once he'd coaxed her out of her shell, she'd happily told him every thought in her head.

They'd both been so young then. So innocent.

Fire burned through him now as he looked at her. *Jasmine.* Her name was like a spell and he could barely stop himself from breathing it aloud. He had to force his face to remain expressionless, his body taut and implacable as if ready for battle.

To attack what? To defend what?

"I'm so pleased you could attend our party at such late notice," Umar continued, placing his hands on Jasmine's shoulders. "We await your permission to serve dinner, my king."

Kareef found himself staring at Umar's possessive

hands on her shoulders. He had the sudden urge to knock them away—to start a brawl with the man who had once saved his life!

But this wasn't just any woman. It was Jasmine. The girl he'd once asked to be his wife.

"Sire?"

"Yes. Dinner." Still clenching his jaw, Kareef motioned to his two bodyguards to attend to the horses. He glanced toward the white pavilion and all the eager waiting faces. Several of the bolder guests were already inching closer to him, trying to catch his eye, hoping to join the conversation. After so many years of solitude in the northern desert of Qais, Kareef was not known for his sociability. But somehow being inaccessible and cold had just made him more desirable to the elite Qusanis of Shafar. Everyone in this godforsaken city seemed desperate for the barbarian king's attention, his favor, his body or his soul.

He wasn't even crowned yet, but according to Qusani tradition they already called him king—and treated him almost like a god. The people of Qusay had seen what he'd done for the desert people of Qais, and wanted that same prosperity for themselves. So they worshipped him.

Kareef hated it. He'd never wanted to come back here. But a few weeks ago, shortly after the death of the old king in a plane crash, his cousin, the crown prince, had abruptly removed himself from the line of succession. Xavian—no, Zafir, Kareef corrected himself, so strange to suddenly call the man he had thought his cousin by a new name!—had learned he had not a single drop of Al'Ramiz blood in his veins, and he'd abdicated the throne. He'd left to jointly rule the nation of Haydar with his wife, Queen Layla.

Zafir's decision had been correct and honorable. Kareef would have approved his actions completely, except for one thing: it had forced him to accept the throne in his place.

And now—he would see Jasmine married to another man before his very eyes.

Or would he? Legally, morally, could he allow it?

He cursed beneath his breath.

"You honor us, sire." Umar Hajjar bowed. "If I may ask another favor…"

Kareef growled a reply.

"Will you do my future bride the honor of escorting her into the pavilion?"

He wanted Kareef to touch her? To take her by the hand? Just looking at Jasmine was torture. She'd once been an enchanting girl with big dark eyes and a willowy figure. Now she'd grown into her curves. She'd become a mature woman. Her expression held mystery and hidden sorrows. A man could look into that face for years and never discover all her secrets.

Jasmine Kouri was, quite simply, the most beautiful woman Kareef had ever seen in his life.

And she continued to look at him silently with her dark gaze, her eyes accusing him of everything her lips did not. Reminding him of everything he'd nearly killed himself to forget.

Kareef closed his eyes, briefly blocking her from his vision. He forced his body to be calm, his breathing to become steady and even. He discarded emotion from his body, brushing it from his soul like dirt off his skin. After so many years of practice, he knew exactly what to do.

Then he opened his eyes and discovered he'd learned nothing.

Looking at Jasmine, years of repressed desire dissolved his will into dust. Heat flashed through him, whipping through his skin like a sandstorm flaying the flesh off his living bones.

He wanted her. He always had. As he'd never wanted any woman.

"Sire?"

Unwillingly, Kareef held out his arm, a mark of the highest respect for another man's bride. When he spoke, his voice was utterly cold and controlled.

"Shall we go in to the banquet, Miss Kouri?"

She hesitated, then placed her hand on his arm. He could feel the heat of her light touch through the fabric of his sleeve. She tilted her head back to look up at him. Her beautiful brown eyes glittered. "You honor me, my king."

No one but Kareef could hear the bitter irony beneath her words.

The party guests stepped back with deep, reverent bows as he led Jasmine up on the dais, Umar following behind them. Once they were on the dais, Kareef dropped her hand. He picked up a gold flute from the table.

Instantly, the two hundred guests went silent, waiting breathlessly for their new king to speak.

"I wish to thank my honored host and friend, Umar Hajjar, for his gracious invitation." He gave his old friend a nod. In response, Umar bowed, elegant in his designer suit. "And I wish to welcome

his future bride, Jasmine Kouri, back to her home-
land. You grace our shores with your beauty, Miss
Kouri." He held up the flute, looking at the guests
with hard eyes as he intoned forcefully, "To the
happy couple."

"To the happy couple," the guests repeated in awed
unison.

Jasmine said nothing. But as they sat down, he
could feel the glow of her hatred pushing against him
in waves of palpable energy.

Dinner was served, a meal of limitless, endless
courses of lamb and fish, of spiced rice and olives and
baked aubergines stuffed with meat. Each dish was
more elaborate than the last. And through it all, Kareef
was aware of Jasmine sitting next to him. She barely
ate, even when encouraged by her fiancé. She just
gripped her fork and knife tightly. Like weapons.

"You should eat, my dear," Umar Hajjar chided her
from the other side. "It would be unattractive for you
to grow too thin."

Unattractive? *Jasmine?*

Kareef frowned. Thin or fat, naked or dressed in a
burlap sack, any man would want her. He clenched his
hands into fists upon the table. *He* wanted her. Right
now. On this table.

No, he told himself fiercely. He wouldn't touch her.
He'd sworn thirteen years ago to leave Jasmine in peace.
And she was now engaged to another man—his friend.

Turning to Umar Hajjar, Kareef forced himself to
speak normally. "I did not know you were friends."

"We met in New York last year." Umar gave her arm
a friendly little squeeze. "After my poor wife died, I

asked Jasmine many times to marry me. She finally accepted yesterday."

"Yesterday? And you plan to wed in a few days?" he said evenly. "A swift engagement. There are no…impediments?"

Jasmine looked at Kareef sharply, with an intake of breath. He did not meet her eyes.

Umar shrugged carelessly. "Any wedding can be arranged quickly, if a man does not care about the cost." He glanced down at Jasmine teasingly. "Beautiful women can be fickle. I'm not going to give this one a chance to change her mind."

Jasmine looked down at her full plate, her cheeks bright red. She ran tracks through her rice with her fork.

"I would have married her immediately, in New York," Umar continued, "but Jasmine wished to be reconciled with her family. After my horse wins the Qais Cup, we will move to America for half the year to pursue my next goal—the Triple Crown. And of course I will take over Jasmine's business in New York. Her only job will be as mother to my four sons. But her connections in America will be useful to me as I…"

He paused when one of his servants bent to whisper in his ear. Abruptly, Umar rose to his feet. "Excuse me. I must take a phone call. With your permission, sire…?"

Kareef gave him a single nod. After he left, as all the guests on the lower floor buzzed loudly with their own discussions, he lowered his head to speak in a low voice to Jasmine alone.

"Does he know?"

Her whole body became strangely still. "Don't even

think about it," she ground out. "It doesn't count. It meant nothing."

"You know you cannot marry him."

"Don't be ridiculous."

"Jasmine."

"No! I don't care if you're king, I won't let you ruin my life—again!" Her eyes flashed at him. "I won't let you ruin my family's hopes with this wedding—"

"Your family needs the wedding?" he interrupted.

Clenching her jaw, she shook her head. "I won't let them be crushed by my old scandal again, not when everyone's still buzzing about my sister!"

"Which sister?"

Staring at him, she exhaled. "You haven't heard? I thought everyone in Qusay knew." She gave a sudden humorless laugh. "My youngest sister Nima was at boarding school in Calista. She had a one-night stand with some sailor whose name she can't even remember. Now she's pregnant. Pregnant at sixteen."

The word *pregnant* floated between them like poisoned air.

Ripping his gaze away, Kareef glanced at her large family, now seated at a lower table. At Umar Hajjar crossing the grass near the tent. At all the guests watching the king surreptitiously beneath the white pavilion. Then he looked back at Jasmine, and it all faded away. He couldn't see anything but the beauty of her face—the endless darkness of her eyes.

"Nima's staying in New York now, living in my apartment, trying to wrap her head around the thought that she will soon be a mother." She blinked back tears. "My baby sister. When she showed up on my doorstep two days ago, I suddenly realized how much time I'd lost. Thirteen years without my family." Her voice cracked. "No money can replace that."

"So you got engaged to Umar Hajjar," he said quietly. He narrowed his eyes. "Do you love him?"

With a sigh, she rubbed her neck. "When my father sent me away thirteen years ago," she whispered, "he said not to bother coming home again. Not until I was a respectable married woman."

Kareef set his jaw, furious as he glared at her. "So that's why you got engaged?" he bit out. "To please your father?"

She looked up at him, hatred suddenly blazing in her eyes.

"What do you care? You washed your hands of me long ago. In a few days I'll be married and out of your life forever." She lifted her chin, and her eyes glittered. "So leave me alone. Go get yourself crowned. Sire."

In all the years he'd known Jasmine, he'd never heard that bitter tone from her lips. But could he blame her? What she'd gone through would make any woman's soul grow brittle. Her young spirit had been so happy and bright, but he'd crushed that long ago. His hands tightened as he leaned forward over the table.

"But Jasmine," he said in a low voice, "you have to know that I—"

"Forgive me," Umar Hajjar interrupted, his voice high and strained. They turned almost guiltily to find him standing behind them. "My children's nanny was on the phone. There is an emergency. I must go."

"Oh no!" Jasmine rose to her feet anxiously. "I will come with you."

Umar held up his hand. "I must go alone."

"What? Why? Please, Umar," she begged. "Let me come with you. You might need my help!"

"No," he said harshly. His eyes fell upon Kareef. "My king, I ask you to take Jasmine under your protection."

"No! Absolutely not!" she cried, too loudly. Guests turned to look.

"Jasmine," Umar cautioned in a low, hard voice, "do not create a scene."

She swallowed. "I won't," she choked out softly. Her dark eyes glimmered, pleading with him as they turned away from the crowd. "Just don't leave me with the king."

"Why?" her fiancé demanded.

She licked her lips, glancing at Kareef beneath trembling lashes. "Though he is king…he is also still a man."

"Don't be foolish, Jasmine. He's the king!" Umar said. "His word is unbreakable. His honor is respected across the world. He—"

"No, she is right," Kareef interrupted. He looked down at Jasmine with glittering eyes. "Though I am king," he said in a low, dangerous voice, "I am also still a man."

Her long, black eyelashes swept across her pale cheeks as she visibly trembled beneath his gaze.

"And I would trust you with my life," Umar said stoutly. "Please. You must take her, sire."

Kareef slowly turned to his old friend. Bring Jasmine back to the royal palace? Beneath the same roof? The gleaming palace already felt like a prison with its thick walls, when Kareef hungered for the wide freedom of the desert. He couldn't imagine being trapped in that gilded cage with the additional torture of Jasmine's company—under his protection as he waited for her to marry another man!

"No," he said coldly. "She cannot stay at the palace. It's impossible."

But even as Jasmine exhaled in relief, Umar pressed his lips together. "She cannot stay unchaperoned here until we are married. It would be improper. I have my children to consider."

"Send her home to her family."

"It will be far more useful if she stays at the palace, my king."

Ah, so this was about status. Kareef's lip twisted with scorn.

"For Jasmine's sake," the other man added in a low voice. "Your attention will go far to negate her old scandal. People will forget the whispers beneath the weight of your honor."

Staring at him, Kareef frowned in sudden indecision.

Umar lowered his head. "My king, if I have ever done anything worthy of your esteem, I beg you this one favor. Place my bride formally under your protection until the day of the Qais Cup, when I will return to marry her."

If he'd ever done anything worthy of Kareef's esteem?

He'd helped Kareef bring prosperity to the desert. Made him the godfather of two of his four young sons. And most of all—he'd found Kareef in the desert, half-mad and dying of thirst thirteen years ago. He'd brought him home, brought him back to health. He'd saved Kareef's life.

"Perhaps…" Kareef said grudgingly, and Umar pounced.

"Your mother is at the palace, is she not, sire? She will make a fine chaperone, if you are concerned about propriety."

"No," Jasmine whimpered softly. "I won't do it."

Umar ignored her. He kept staring at Kareef with hope—almost desperation.

If the bride had been any other woman, Kareef would have immediately agreed. But not *this* woman. He cursed beneath his breath. Damn it, didn't the man see the risk?

No, of course he did not. Umar had no idea Kareef was the one who'd taken her virginity and caused her accident in the desert thirteen years ago. No one knew Kareef was the man who'd been her lover, her partner in the scandal. Jasmine had made sure of that.

She still hated him. He saw it in her eyes. But he had no choice.

Slowly, Kareef rose to his feet. His voice was loud, ringing with authority beneath the white pavilion.

"As of this moment, and until the day of her marriage, Jasmine Kouri is under my protection."

Another buzz rose across the crowd. They stared at Jasmine with awe. Even her old father cracked an amazed smile.

If only he knew the truth, Kareef thought grimly.

Nodding in relief, Umar turned to go.

"Wait," Jasmine cried, grabbing her fiancé's slender wrist. "I still don't know what's happened! Are your children sick? Is it the baby?"

"The children are well. I cannot say more." The older man's eyes were narrow and tight. "I will call you if I can. Otherwise—I will see you at the race. On our wedding day."

And he was gone. Kareef and Jasmine sat alone on the dais, with two hundred pairs of eyes upon them.

Keeping his face impassive, Kareef threw down the linen napkin across his empty plate and glanced at Jasmine's untouched dinner and stricken, forlorn face. "Are you finished?"

"Yes," she whispered miserably, as if she were trying not to cry.

He held out his hand. "Then let us go."

She focused her eyes on him. "Forget it. I've been under my own *protection* for years. I do not need or want yours."

He continued to hold out his hand. "And yet you have it."

"I will go stay at my family's house."

"Your betrothed wishes otherwise."

"He is not the boss of me."

"Is he not?"

She tossed her head. "I will stay at a hotel."

She was trying her best to be insolent, making it clear she did not respect him. He should have been insulted, but as he watched the tip of her pink tongue dart out to lick her lips, he couldn't look away from the lush, sensual mouth he'd kissed long ago. It seemed like only yesterday. His lips tingled, remembering hers.

With a deep breath, he forced himself to look up. "You will find no available hotel room, anywhere on this island. All the world has come for my coronation." He tightened his jaw. "But that is not the point."

"And that is?"

"I gave my word to Hajjar," he ground out. "And I keep my promises."

"Do you?" Her eyes glinted at him sardonically. "A new skill?"

Anger flashed through him. But he held it back, dousing it with ice. He deserved the jibe. He would accept it from Jasmine as he would from no other person alive.

He would still prevail.

"Are you afraid to be near me?" he quietly taunted.

"Afraid of you?" Her voice shimmered with hatred like moonlight on water. "Why should I be?"

He held out his hand. "Then come."

Narrowing her eyes at him in fury, she pushed her hand into his. She never could resist a dare. But the same instant he knew he'd won, he felt the electric shock of her touch. And realized he was the one who should be afraid.

He, Kareef Al'Ramiz, the prince of the desert, soon to be absolute ruler of the kingdom of Qusay, should be afraid of what he'd do when left alone with this woman he craved. This woman he could not have. His friend's betrothed. Because Jasmine wasn't simply a woman to him.

She was the only woman.

CHAPTER TWO

TWILIGHT was falling over the gleaming towers and spires of the royal palace overlooking the city. Built over the ruins of a Byzantine citadel, the palace had been modernized in the last century and could be seen for miles across the Mediterranean, shining like a jewel.

So strange to be back here, Jasmine thought, in the place she'd grown up when her father had been the old king's favored counselor. Although this was the first time she'd ever been in this particular wing. The maid had left her in a shabby garret in the oldest wing of the palace, where the servants lived.

Jasmine looked out through the grimy window toward the garden. This room was smaller than the walk-in closet of her Park Avenue penthouse, but all she felt was relief to be alone.

Her knees were still weak with shock as she hefted her small rolling suitcase on the single bed. When Kareef had led her away from the white pavilion to his waiting limousine, she'd been half-terrified that he would take her straight to his bedroom in the palace. Would she have been able to resist—even hating him as she did?

The thought was still staggering. After so many years, she'd seen Kareef again. Heard his voice. Felt his touch.

The air in the room felt suddenly stifling. She punched buttons on the control panel of the air-conditioning, then gave up and tried to open the window, but the glass wouldn't budge.

Cursing aloud, she covered her face with her hands. Why had she ever come back to the palace? Because she was obeying Umar's orders? She'd survived on her own in New York City for thirteen years. She did not need or want Kareef's *protection*!

Or did she?

Against her will, she remembered the touch of Kareef's hand against her own and felt like she was burning up with a fever. Sweating, she yanked off the chiffon dress. She wrenched off her stockings and sandals. Standing in just her white bra and panties, she felt relief.

Until there was a hard knock and the door swung open.

"Jasmine—"

Kareef stood in the door. He sucked in his breath when he saw her in the middle of her bedroom, half-naked.

With a stifled scream, she grabbed the chiffon dress off the floor to cover herself. "What are you doing here?"

He stared at her, clenching his hands into fists at his sides. He was no longer in white robes, but more casually dressed in a long-sleeved white shirt and black pants. He looked more devastating than ever, and his towering body was taut. "I want…I want you to join me for a late supper."

"So call me on the phone and ask!" she cried. A servant passed by in the hallway, trying not to gawk. Frowning, Kareef stepped inside the room, closing the door behind him.

"You can't come in here!" she said, scandalized.

"I can't let anyone else see you like this."

"Anyone? What about *you*?"

Lifting a dark eyebrow, he looked her over slowly. "I've seen far more of you than this."

Her cheeks flamed red-hot—and she truly wanted to kill him! "We can't be alone in a closed bedroom! In some parts of the country, you would be required to marry me!"

He gave a low laugh. "It's a good thing we're in the city, then."

"Don't you dare! Don't you realize how gossip can spread?"

"My servants can be trusted."

She shook her head fiercely. "How do you know?"

"One servant betrayed us, Jasmine. One." His eyes glinted. "And I made him pay. Marwan—"

"I'm not going to argue with you!" she nearly shrieked, grabbing a pillow off her bed and lifting it over her head. The dress fell to the floor but she barely noticed. Modesty was inconsequential compared to the blaze of her fury. "Just get out!"

He looked at her body in the white cotton bra and panties. She felt his gaze upon her bare skin from her collarbone to the curve of her breasts, down her flat belly to her naked thighs. Her mouth went dry.

Then, slowly, he met her gaze. "You're threatening me with a pillow, Jasmine?"

Since he was a foot taller and probably eighty pounds heavier than her, she could see why that would seem like a joke. It only made her more angry. "Do you need a handwritten request? Get out!"

"When you agree to join me for dinner."

Staring at him, a jittery nervousness pulsed through her. The last time she'd seen Kareef, he'd been barely eighteen, the king's eldest nephew, slender and tall and fine. She'd been the bookish eldest daughter of the king's adviser; he'd been a wild, reckless horse racer with a vulnerable heart and joyful laugh.

But he'd changed since then. He was no longer a boy; he'd become a man. A dangerous one.

His once-friendly blue eyes were now ruthless; the formerly vibrant expression on his handsome, rugged face had become tightly controlled. His once-lanky frame had gained strength. Even the muscle of his body proclaimed him a king. He could probably pick up someone like Umar and toss him through the air like a javelin. She'd never seen any man on earth with shoulders like Kareef's.

But the biggest change was the grim darkness she now saw beneath his gaze. She could sense the cold warrior hidden beneath his deeply tanned skin. He had only the thinnest veneer of civilization left. The danger both attracted her…and frightened her.

It doesn't matter, she told herself desperately. In a few days she would become Umar's wife and she would never have to see Kareef again. If she could just make it to her wedding…

"So you'll join me?" he said coldly.

"I'm not hungry."

"Come anyway. We have…something to discuss."

"No," she said desperately. "We don't."

He lowered a dark eyebrow. "Do I really have to say it?"

She swallowed. No. She knew exactly what he was talking about. She'd just told herself many times that it didn't matter, that it didn't count, that it had just been a few whispered words between kisses.

The pillow dropped from her hands. She wrapped her arms around her body, glancing toward the deepening shadows of the garden. She whispered, "It's all in the past."

"The past is always with us." Out of the corner of her eye, she saw him take a single step toward her. "You know you cannot marry him."

Oh my God, Kareef was going to touch her! If he did—if he reached out and took her hand—she was afraid of how her body would react. Only her anger was keeping her hands wrapped around her own waist, when some uncivilized part of her longed to stroke the dark curl of his hair, the roughness of his jawline, to touch the hard muscles and discover the man he had become….

With a harsh intake of breath, she held up her hand sharply, keeping him at a distance.

"All right!" she bit out. "I'll join you for your fancy dinner if you'll just leave!"

His blue eyes held hers. "It won't be fancy. Simple and quiet."

"Right." She didn't believe him for a second. She'd never seen any Al'Ramiz king dine with fewer than fifty people and ten courses of meat and fish and fruit.

"The blue room." He looked her over, and she felt

that same flush of heat as his gaze touched her naked skin. "Ten minutes."

The blue room? Now she knew he was lying. The blue room was for entertaining heads of state! But she'd worry about that later—when she wasn't naked and confined with him in such a small space! Unwillingly, her eyes fell on the tiny bed between them.

He followed her gaze.

Suddenly, her heart was pounding so loud she could almost hear it. Then he turned toward the door.

"See you at dinner."

"Yes." She could suddenly breathe again.

He paused, as his large frame filled the doorway. "It's good to see you, Jasmine." And he closed the door behind him.

Good to see her?

As soon as he was gone, she dug frantically through her suitcase and found nothing at all to wear. She lifted up the crumpled green chiffon dress from the floor only to discover a stain on the bodice.

Why was Kareef doing this to her? Why couldn't they just ignore the past? Why couldn't they just pretend it did not exist?

You know you cannot marry him.

She took a deep breath. They'd share one meal. He would speak a few careful words, and it would be done. They could both go on with their lives.

She grabbed a white sundress, fresh and pretty with a modest neckline. It wasn't nearly fancy enough for a fifty-person banquet in the blue room with the king, but it would just have to do. She added sandals and a string of pearls. All sweet and simple, and *hers*. Not selected for her by Umar from a designer boutique. She brushed her long hair, and looked at herself in the mirror.

Bewildered brown eyes looked back at her. She looked young and insecure, nothing like the powerful woman she'd become in New York. Being close to Kareef made her feel vulnerable again. As if she were sixteen.

Her feet dragged as she left her room and headed toward the east wing. The hallways were oddly quiet but she passed two women as she made her way to the blue room—the Sheikha, Kareef's mother, and her much younger companion trailing behind in her black abaya. The Sheikha saw Jasmine and her wrinkled, kindly face lifted into a vague, benevolent smile. She probably didn't remember who Jasmine was. Jasmine bowed deeply.

When she looked up, she saw the Sheikha's companion smiling down at her. It was Sera, her childhood friend! But the Sheikha was in a hurry. Sera had only time to whisper, "Glad you're back," before she had to quickly follow her employer down the hall.

A surprised smile rose on Jasmine's face as she stared after her old friend. Sera still remembered her after all these years? A surge of happiness went through Jasmine, then she turned back to hurry down the hall. The palace seemed strangely silent, almost desolate. Had the big fancy dinner been canceled? Was she late? With a deep breath, Jasmine pushed open the double doors.

The long dining table, big enough to seat forty-eight, was lit by long-tapered candles. Only one person was seated there.

"Jasmine." Kareef rose to his feet with a short, formal bow. He moved to the place beside his at the table, standing behind her chair. "Please."

Shocked, she looked right and left. "Where is everyone else?"

"There is no one else."

"Oh."

"I told you. Simple and quiet."

She was having dinner with Kareef…alone? Feeling like she was in a surreal dream, she walked toward the table. The candles flickered light and shadow upon the white wainscoting and pale blue walls of the cavernous room. She swallowed, then lowered herself into her chair. He pushed it forward for her. As if they were on a date.

No—she couldn't think that way! This was the *opposite* of a date!

Kareef sat down in the chair beside her, then nodded regally at two servants who appeared from the shadows. She jumped as they took silver lids off trays to serve two exquisite meals of cool salad, cucumbers, exquisite fruits, bread and cheeses. They opened a bottle of sparkling water, then a bottle of expensive French wine. After serving the trays, they backed away with a bow and disappeared, closing the double doors softly behind them.

They were alone. And Jasmine felt it. She licked her lips nervously. "What is all this?"

Kareef leaned forward to pour her a glass of wine. "You didn't eat at your engagement party. You must be hungry." His sensual lips quirked. "I allow no one to starve while under my protection."

She watched him, involuntarily noticing the way the candlelight cast shadows across the astonishing masculine beauty of his face.

He looked up, and his blue eyes sizzled through hers with the intensity of his gaze. "Are you?"

"Am I what?" she stammered.

"Are. You. Hungry," he said with slow deliberation, and she found herself looking at his lips and remembering the last time he'd kissed her. So long ago. Or was it? It seemed like it was yesterday, and all the long years since had just been a dream. "Jasmine."

With an intake of breath, she looked up. "Starving," she whispered.

He smiled, then indicated her plate. "One of the few perks of being king," he said. "A world-class chef at my beck and call. A far cry from what I'm used to at my home in Qais."

She took a bite of the food and noticed it was indeed delicious, and she was indeed starving. But as she ate, she couldn't look away from Kareef's face.

Oh, this was dangerous. She couldn't trust him. He'd betrayed her! Ruined her! But her body didn't seem to care. Every time he looked at her, she trembled from within.

She set down her fork. "Kareef. I don't want to be here with you, any more than you want me here. So if you'll just do what must be done—"

"Later," he interrupted. He pushed the crystal goblet full of ruby-colored wine toward her. "We have all night."

All night. Trembling, she took a bracing gulp of wine and wiped her mouth. "But with your coronation in a few days," she stammered, "you must have many demands on your time. I heard something about fireworks tonight, given by the city council in your honor—"

"Nothing is more important—" he refilled her wine-glass "—than this."

Why was he stretching this out? Why? What possible reason could he have?

Helplessly, she took another sip of wine. Silence fell in the shadows of flickering candlelight as they ate.

He glanced at her enormous diamond ring, heavy as a paperweight on her hand. "An expensive trinket, even for a billionaire," he said. "Hajjar values you high."

Embarrassed heat flooded her cheeks. "I'm not marrying him for his money, if that's what you think!"

Something like a smile passed briefly over Kareef's face. "No," he said. "I know you are not."

What was that smile hiding? Some private joke?

Once, she'd known him so well. The boy she'd loved had hidden nothing from her. But she did not know this man.

She watched him take a sip of wine. There was something sensual about watching his lips on the crystal glass, his tongue tasting the red Bordeaux. She could almost imagine those lips, that tongue, upon her body.

No! she ordered herself desperately. *Stop it!*

But every inch of her skin shivered with awareness that she was sitting beside the only man she'd ever loved.

The only man she'd ever hated.

"Do you like New York?" he asked, taking a bite of fruit.

"Yes," she said, watching his sharp teeth crunch the flesh of the apple. "I did."

"But you're eager to leave it."

She looked away. "I missed Qusay. I missed my family."

"But you must have made many friends in New York."

There was something strange beneath his tone. She looked back at him. "Of course."

His tone was light, even as his hand tightened around the neck of the goblet. "Such an exciting city. You must have enjoyed the nightlife frequently with many ardent…friends."

Was that an oblique way of asking if she'd taken lovers? With a deep breath, she took another sip of wine. She wasn't going to tell him he'd been her only lover. It would be too pathetic to admit she'd spent the best years of her life alone, dreaming of him against her will. Especially since she knew he'd replaced her the instant he'd left her. She wouldn't give Kareef the satisfaction of knowing he'd been not just her first—but her only!

Taking a bite of salad, so delicious with its herbs and spices and multicolored tomatoes, she deliberately changed the subject. "What's your home like?"

He snorted. "The palace? It has not changed. A rich and luxurious prison."

"I mean your house in the desert. In Qais."

Taking another sip of wine, he blinked then shrugged. "Comfortable. A few servants, but they're mostly for the horses. I like to take care of myself. I don't like people hovering."

She nearly laughed. "You must love being king."

"No." His voice was flat. "But it is my duty."

Duty, she thought with sudden fury. Where had his

sense of duty been thirteen years ago, when she'd needed him so desperately and he'd abandoned her?

Anger pulsed through her, making her hands shake as she held her knife and fork. But it wasn't just anger, she realized. It was bewilderment and pain. How could he have done it? How?

Placing her hands in her lap, she turned her head away, blinking fast.

"Jasmine, what is it?"

"Nothing," she said hoarsely. She would die before she let Kareef Al'Ramiz see her weep. She'd learned to be strong. She'd had no other choice. "I just remember you once dreamed of a house in the desert. Now you have it."

"Yes." His voice suddenly hardened. "And I will be your neighbor. My home is but thirty kilometers from Umar Hajjar's estate."

She turned with an intake of breath at mention of her fiancé's name. Oh God, how could she have already forgotten Umar? She was an engaged woman! She shouldn't be looking at another man's lips!

But she could not stop herself. Not when the man was Kareef, the only man she'd ever loved. The only man she'd ever taken to her bed. And until yesterday—the only man she'd ever kissed.

Umar had kissed her for the first time only after she'd accepted his marriage proposal. His kiss had been businesslike and official, a pledge to seal the deal when a handshake wouldn't do. He did not seem particularly keen to sweep her immediately into bed, which was just fine with Jasmine. Their marriage would be based on something far more important:

family. And she wasn't just getting back her parents and sisters. She would finally be a mother. She would help to raise his young sons, aged two to fourteen.

"Do you know his children?" she asked thickly.

He nodded. "I am godfather to his two eldest—Fadi and Bishr. They are good children. Respectful."

Respectful? They hadn't seemed that way when she'd met them last year in New York—at least not respectful to Jasmine. The four boys had glared at her, clinging to their father and their French nanny, Léa, as if Jasmine were the enemy. She sighed. But who could blame them for being upset, when their mother had just died?

"I hope they're all right," she whispered. "I met them only once. His poor children. They've had a hard time. Especially the baby," she added, looking away.

"They need a mother," Kareef said softly. "You will be good to them."

She looked at him with an intake of breath. He leaned across the table, his gaze intense in the candlelight. He was already so close, his knee just inches from hers.

"Thank you," she said softly. Sadness settled around her heart as unspoken memories stretched between them.

"Didn't you know she was pregnant, my lord?" the doctor's voice echoed in her ears, from the dark cave long ago. *"She'll live, but never be able to conceive again...."*

Remembering, Jasmine dropped her silver fork with a clatter against her china plate. Clasping her hands tightly in her lap, she tried to close off the memories from her mind.

"You've always wanted children," Kareef said. There was a grim set to his jaw. "And now you're to be married to Umar Hajjar. A fine match by any measure. Your father must be proud."

"Yes. Now," she whispered. She shook her head. "He's never cared about my success in New York. He even refused the money I've tried to send the family, as his fortunes have faltered while mine have grown." She lifted her gaze. "But I've always believed some corner of his heart wanted to forgive me. My success in large part came from him!"

Kareef shifted in his chair.

She continued. "When I first arrived in New York at sixteen, I had nothing. No money. My only friend there was an elderly great-aunt, and she was ill. Not just ill—dying. In a rat-infested apartment."

"I heard," he said quietly. "Later."

She narrowed her eyes at him, feeling a surge of bitterness. "I worked three jobs to support us both. Then," she whispered, "out of the blue the month before she died, I got a check from my father for fifty thousand dollars. It saved us. I invested every penny, and gradually it paid off. But if not for him," she said softly, "I might still be an office cleaner working sixteen hours a day."

He picked up his glass, taking a sip of wine.

Jasmine frowned, tilting her head. "But when I tried to thank my father for that money today, he claimed not to know anything about it."

Kareef stared idly at the ruby-colored wine, swirling it in the candlelight.

And suddenly, she knew.

"My father never sent that money, did he?"

He didn't answer.

She sucked in her breath. "It was you," she whispered. "You sent me that money ten years ago. Not my father. It was you."

Pressing his lips together, he set down the glass. He gave a single hard nod.

"The letter said it was from my father."

"I didn't think you would accept it from me."

"You're right!"

"So I lied."

"You…lied. Just like that?"

"I intended to send you more every year, but you never needed it." Kareef's voice held a tinge of pride as he looked at her. "You turned that first small amount into a fortune."

"Why did you do it, Kareef?"

He turned to look at her. "Don't you know?"

She shook her head.

Reaching over the table, he took her hand in his own. Turning it over, he kissed her palm.

A tremor racked her body, coursing through her like an electric current, lit up by the caress of his lips against her skin.

He looked up at her. His blue eyes were endless, like the sea in the flickering light. "Because you're my wife, Jasmine."

Silence filled the blue room, broken by sudden booms of fireworks outside, rattling the windowpanes.

She snatched back her hand. "No, I'm not!"

"You spoke the words," he said evenly. "So did I."

"It wasn't legal. There were no witnesses."

"It doesn't matter, not according to the laws of Qais."

"It would never hold up in the civil courts of Qusay."

"We are married."

Through the high arched windows, she saw fireworks lighting the dark sky. Struggling to collect her thoughts, she shook her head. "Abandonment could be considered reason for divorce—"

He looked at her. "Your abandonment?" he said quietly. "Or mine?"

She sucked in her breath. "I was forced to leave Qusay! It was never of my free will!"

He looked at her. "I had cause to leave you as well."

Yeah. Right. Her eyes glittered at him. "We were barely more than children. We didn't know what we were doing."

As the explosions continued to spiral across the night sky, booming like thunder, he leaned forward and stroked her face.

"I knew," he said in a low voice. "And so did you."

The tension altered, humming with a hot awareness that coiled and stretched between them.

Her cheek sizzled where he stroked her. His gaze dropped to her mouth. She felt her body tighten. Her breasts suddenly ached, her nipples taut with longing.

No!

"If we once were married," she choked out, "speak the words to undo it now. All I care about now…is my family."

"And what of you?" he said, cupping her face in his strong hands. "What do you want for yourself?"

She wanted him to kiss her. Wanted it with every ounce of her blood and beat of her heart.

But she wouldn't allow this insane desire to destroy the life that was finally within reach, the family life she hungered to have. She lifted her dark lashes to look into his eyes. "I want a home." Her voice was as quiet as the whisper of memory. "A family. I want a husband and children of my own."

A loud crash boomed in the night sky outside them, shaking the palace.

Kareef looked down at her, his eyes suddenly dark as a midnight sea. He dropped his hands from her face. "Umar Hajjar loves his children, his horses and his money—in that order," he said harshly. "As his wife, you will be valued a distant fourth on his list."

"He values my connections in America. He thinks I will be the perfect wife—the perfect hostess. That is enough."

"Not enough for him."

"What else could he want from me?"

He looked at her.

"You're a beautiful woman," he said thickly. "No man could resist you."

She stared up at him for several heartbeats, then turned away, hiding her face.

"That's not true," she said in a low voice. "One man has had no trouble resisting me, Kareef." She looked up. "You."

He grabbed her wrist on the table. His fingers tightened on her skin. "You think I don't want you?"

His voice was dangerous. Low. She felt tension snapping between them, rippling through her body, sharp against every nerve.

Her heart beat frantically in her chest. As he leaned toward her, she breathed in his masculine scent, laced with the flavor of wine and spice. His body, in all its strength and power, was so close to hers. She yearned to lean across the table, to lose everything in one moment of sweet madness and press her mouth against his....

Another loud boom exploded outside. It broke the spell. Made her realize she was perilously close to doing something unforgivable.

Rising to her feet, she stumbled back from the table.

"Divorce me," she whispered. "If you've ever cared about me, Kareef, if I was ever more than a warm body in the night to you...divorce me tonight."

He stared at her, his jaw tight. Then he shook his head. Tears rose to her eyes and she fought them with all her might.

"You bastard," she choked out. "You cold-hearted bastard. I've known for years you had no heart, but I never thought you could...never thought you would—"

But the tears were starting to fall from her lashes. Turning before he could see them, she shoved open the double doors. They banged loudly against the walls as she fled down the hallway.

"Jasmine! Stop!"

But she didn't obey. She just ran.

Fireworks boomed outside the tall windows as she raced past the corner where she'd first crashed into Kareef—literally—by sliding on the marble floors in her socks, playing with her sisters. When she slid too fast around the corner, he'd grasped her wrists, catching her before she could fall. His blue eyes had smiled down at her with the warmth of spring's first sun. She'd loved him from that first day.

Now, after thirteen years of trying to forget Kareef's existence, this one day had brought it all back, times ten. A single word from his deep voice, a single look from his handsome face, and he'd caught up Jasmine's soul like a fish in his net.

Racing down the hall, she pushed open the first door on her left and ran down the wooden stairs into the courtyard. Cloaked in darkness, she took deep rattling gasps of the warm desert air. She stood beneath the swaying dark palm trees of the garden, beside the dark water shimmering in the silvery moonlight, and wrapped her arms over her thin cotton sundress. She could not allow herself to cry. She could not allow herself to collapse.

Because this time, if she fell, there would be no prince to catch her.

CHAPTER THREE

KAREEF nearly staggered in shock as Jasmine fled the dining room. Jasmine thought he didn't want her? *Didn't she know her power?*

When he heard the double doors bang behind her, he leapt to his feet. With an intake of breath, he pursued her. He saw her disappear through a wooden door in the hallway. The door to the royal garden, forbidden to all but the king's family. He followed her outside.

He stopped at the foot of the stairs, turning his face up to the night sky. He heard an owl's distant echoing cry. He felt the warm desert wind against his face, blowing open his white shirt.

He was on the hunt. He no longer felt like a king, constrained by the rigid boundaries of duty and appearance. Suddenly, he felt wild. Uncontrolled. For the first time since he'd returned to the palace in Shafar, he felt like himself again.

No. It had been longer than that since he'd truly felt like himself. Far longer…

Where was she? He looked to the right and left, searching across the dark shadows of trees and shimmering pools of water like a Qusani hawk seeking his prey. Had she disappeared into the night? Did she truly exist only in dreams?

The moonlight cast a silvery glow on the swaying palm trees. He could hear the wind through the leaves, hear the burbling water of the fountain. In the distance, he could hear the Mediterranean pounding beneath the cliffs.

Booms like cannons ricocheted with increasing vigor across the sky. Explosions spiraled like pale flowers of smoke across the night—fireworks provided by the city of Shafar to celebrate his coming coronation. He knew he should be thanking the city council right now, instead of pursuing this ghost from his past—this woman who'd given herself freely to another man.

But not yet. She was still his. *She was still his.*

He saw a sudden flash of white. He saw her lithe body cross the garden, darting and shimmering between the dark shadows. Silvery moonlight twisted through her onyx hair, causing her short, filmy white gown to glow. She was a creature of seduction, a faerie creature of the night, illuminating it like any man's fantasy.

Jasmine. How long had he hungered for her? How long had he thirsted, like a man crossing oceans of hot sand?

He stood still, watching her in the moonlight. Afraid to breathe, lest the dream disappear.

His expression hardened as he moved forward.

Too many years of hunger. Too many years of denied desire.

She wished to have her freedom. He would give it to her. But not yet.

Tonight, she was still his.

For this night, she was his to possess.

As he caught up with her, he saw her long dark hair tumbling down her pale, bare shoulders in the moonlight. Shoulders now shaking with silent sobs.

A branch snapped into the grass beneath his foot as he stopped abruptly.

She didn't turn around, but he knew she'd heard him by the sudden stiffening of her posture.

"I know I shouldn't be here." Her voice was sodden, muffled. "Have you come to kick me out?"

Grabbing her shoulder, he turned her around. "This garden is forbidden to all but the royal family."

"I know—"

"And you are my wife."

She looked up at him with a gasp. Her eyes were wide and dark, her tears glimmering in the moonlight like endless pools. "But I can't be," she choked out. "You are the king. And I must marry—"

"I know." His eyes searched hers. "I will give you your divorce, Jasmine."

"You will?"

"Yes," he said in a low voice. "But not yet."

"What do you want from me?" she whispered.

His hand tightened on her bare shoulder. What did he want?

He wanted to strip the flimsy dress off her body and lay her down beneath him in the moist, cool grass. He wanted to close his eyes and feel her wholly in his grasp, to feel the beat of her heart and warmth of her skin.

He wanted to kiss her senseless, to lick and suckle every inch of her naked body, from that slender, delicate neck to her full breasts, down her tiny waist to the wide sweep of her hips.

He wanted to dip his tongue into every crevice of her, to taste and bite every delicious curve. To savor the spicy sweetness of her skin until he could bear it no longer, while he plunged himself into her so hard and deeply that he would never resurface again.

Part of him—the civilized part—knew it was wrong. Jasmine was another man's betrothed. And she was under his protection.

But as he held her in his arms…Kareef was no longer a civilized man.

"You," he growled in reply. "I want you."

"No," she gasped. Her brown eyes shimmered with fear. "We can't!"

He breathed in her scent of spice and blood oranges and something more, something distinctly her, the intoxicating feminine warmth of her skin. He smelled the fragrant night-blooming jasmine, and he didn't bother to answer. He just lowered his head to kiss her.

With a jagged intake of breath, she turned her head away, toward the darkness of the trees.

He put his hand on her cheek. "Look at me, Jasmine." She stubbornly refused.

"Look at me!" He twisted his hands into her hair, forcing her compliance. He lifted her chin, looking down into her face. "You are my wife. You cannot refuse what we both desire."

She took a deep breath, then closed her eyes. Moonlight illuminated a trail of tears streaking down her pale skin.

"No," she whispered, trembling in his hands. "I cannot deny what you say."

He felt her surrender. Gloried in it. His calloused hand stroked her bare arm. Her skin felt soft, so soft beneath his fingertips. Just touching her face, as he breathed in her delicious scent, caused a sizzle like fire to spread through his veins. He felt her shudder beneath his touch.

Kareef was king of the land, but there was one thing that had always been beyond his control. One thing that had always been more powerful than his own strength.

His desire for her.

She made his blood boil with longing. Her memory had driven him half-mad with the unsatisfied desire of thirteen years.

And now…she was in his arms.

He looked down at Jasmine's beautiful face with a shudder of longing. Holding her close, he cupped her chin. Lowering his head, he kissed her closed eyelids with a feather-light brush of his lips.

Then, with a hunger he could barely control, he slowly lowered his mouth toward hers. He paused, his lips inches from her own. Then he ruthlessly kissed her, searing her lips with his.

Jasmine gasped as he kissed her.

The hot dark pleasure of his embrace was beyond every fantasy of her endless lonely nights. As his lips crushed hers, she felt herself slide beneath the waves of her longing. Even as she knew it was wrong, she felt herself drowning in desire.

Kareef. Her husband. She could not resist him. She

could not deny him. Body and soul, she felt herself pulled down, down, down into the consuming passion of his savage embrace.

His lips plundered hers with power and skill. As his tongue swept her mouth, entwining with hers, she sagged in his arms, shaking with explosive need. Her knees were weak, but every other part of her was taut and tense. Her nipples tightened painfully, her breasts aching and heavy. Nerve endings sizzled down her body, coiling low in her belly.

She was breathless, helpless with desire. He possessed her as no man ever had.

Then his kiss somehow changed. His lips gentled against hers, and she wasn't just submitting to his power. She was kissing him back. His sensual mouth moved against hers in a languorous dance, and every part of her body beneath her thin dress felt on fire where he pressed against her. She was fragile against the hardness of his chest, and the muscles of his thighs strained against her own. He held her so tightly she no longer knew where she ended and he began, and she realized she'd wrapped her arms around his neck.

A soft cry came from deep inside her, a gasp for breath. Her head fell back, exposing her neck. He pressed small intense kisses along her throat, sending sparks up and down her body. He caressed her body, whispering words of tenderness in the ancient dialect of Qais before suckling the tender flesh of her earlobes. His hands moved against her bare arms, cupping the full breasts that strained toward him beneath the fabric.

How long had she desired this? How long had she told herself she would never feel this way again—that at twenty-nine she was too old, too used-up, too numb to ever feel such pleasure? How long had she told herself she should settle for being useful, for earning money, for trying to be a good daughter, a good sister, a good wife?

Hands in her hair, Kareef whispered ancient words of longing and tenderness against her skin. Around them, she was dimly aware of dappled moonlight through the dark waving silhouettes of palm trees, of the stars scattered across the violet night. They were entwined in each other.

Kareef. The only one who'd ever made her feel such explosive joy. The only one who'd made her feel the night was magic, and life as infinite as the stars above her.

Opening her eyes, she stared at him. She saw the new tiny crinkles at his eyes, the way his shoulders had broadened with muscle. He'd grown into his full strength, with a warrior's posture and brutal power.

But his smile hadn't changed. His voice hadn't changed.

His kiss hadn't changed.

As he lowered his mouth to hers, every inch of her skin sparked with awareness, as if there were a magnetic attraction between them. Pulling them together. Forcing them apart.

Everything else might have altered in their lives, but somehow in his embrace, time stood still. She was sixteen again. They were in love, in longing, full of faith for the future.

That feeling was the most dangerous thing of all.

She shuddered, and with all her strength, she pushed him away.

"I can't," she choked out. Above them, she could hear only the waving palm fronds, the sigh of the wind, the plaintive cries of night birds. "I'm sorry."

"Sorry?" Kareef's voice was barely more than a growl in the darkness. "I am the one to blame. I wanted you then." Reaching down, he caressed her cheek and whispered, "I want you now."

The timbre of his low voice, sharp and deep, caused a seismic shift inside her, breaking her apart in bits like the emeralds hacked from Qusani mines beneath the earth. Gleaming facets and chinks of her soul scattered beneath his touch.

She closed her eyes as she felt his rough fingertips against her cheek. She felt his thumb slide lightly across her sensitive lower lip. Her mouth parted, her body ached, from her nipples down her belly and lower still.

"I will make you a wife, Jasmine," he whispered, stroking her cheek. "I will make you a mother."

Her eyes flew open. He was looking down at her with intensity, his face so boyishly handsome it took her breath away. As teenagers, they'd had many innocent trysts in this very garden so long ago, in another life. But here in the warmth of the desert night, with the spice of the air sifting the salt from the sea, anything seemed possible.

"What do you mean?" she said in shock, searching his eyes.

"If Umar Hajjar is the man you want to marry," he said, "I will not stop you. I will give you away at the wedding myself."

A lump of pain rose in her throat. Oh. "You will?"

His sensual lips spread into a half smile, his eyes heavy with desire. "But not yet."

She trembled.

From a distance she heard a servant calling for the king. She tried to pull her hand away. "I have to go."

The cell phone in his hip pocket started to buzz. Even here in the forbidden garden, they were not completely alone. But he ignored it. As she tried to pull away, he tightened his hand on hers. "Come with me where no one can reach us. Come with me to the desert."

She shook her head desperately. "I have no reason to go anywhere with you!"

He pulled her close against his chest, looking down at her. His face was inches from her own and suddenly she couldn't breathe. He looked down at her, brushing tendrils of hair off her face.

"Are you sure?" he said in a low voice. "Absolutely no reason to be alone with me?"

"Yes," she breathed, hardly able to know what she was saying. "No."

He suddenly leaned back on his hip. "Surely you're not afraid?"

Terrified was more like it, but she would never admit that in a million years. "I'm not afraid of you. I've never been afraid of you!"

"So there's no reason to refuse. We'll leave tomorrow."

When he touched her, she had a difficult time concentrating. "Why—why would you take me to the desert?"

He gave her a slow-rising smile. "You're under my…protection. I take you as my duty."

She stared at that sensual smile. How could he be so cruel? Didn't he realize how desire tormented her?

No, how could he? His bed was likely filled with a new woman every night.

As he stroked her cheek, she looked up at him with pleading eyes. "No," she choked out. "I won't go."

"I can't divorce you unless we go to the desert," he said quietly, looking down at her. "The jewel is there."

She blinked. The emerald. Of course they needed that for their divorce.

And to think she'd actually imagined he was going to whisk her off to the desert for some kind of seduction. Ridiculous. Even if Kareef wanted her, he wouldn't take a long journey across the country just to seduce the woman he'd abandoned years ago. Not when half the women of this city were eagerly begging for the new king to sample their charms!

She truly had lost her mind to think she'd be that special to him. But still—the idea of being alone with him frightened her. "You have so many diplomatic duties here for your coming coronation," she said. "Surely you can send someone to get it?"

"There are some things a man prefers to do himself," he said evenly. "Even if he is king." He raised a dark eyebrow. "And I'm taking you with me."

She licked her lips. "All...all right."

She couldn't leave any question mark that might cast doubt on the legality of her new marriage to Umar. What choice did she have?

A slightly hysterical bubble of laughter escaped her. She could just imagine her father's face if he found out that she was married to the king!

"What is making you smile?" Kareef demanded.

"I was just imagining my father's face if I told him we'd been married for the last thirteen years. Do you think he'd find that respectable enough?"

Kareef paused, then laughed with her in a deep baritone, his eyes bright. "And Hajjar would find a way to incorporate the royal Qusani coat of arms onto his flag, or at least his business card."

For a moment, they grinned at each other.

Then Jasmine's smile faded. "Except no one must ever know I've been your wife."

His eyes darkened. "Because?"

"There must be no scandal against the new king's name. Not after the grief of your uncle's death—the shock of your cousin's abdication." She shook her head. "The people of Qusay have been through enough in the last few weeks to last a lifetime." She took a deep breath, raising her eyes to his. "And you must think of your bride."

He frowned. "My bride? What bride?"

"The bride you will soon take, in your duty as king."

He stared at her, clenching his jaw.

"A royal princess," she said. "With a perfect reputation."

He looked away.

"A beautiful virgin to give you children," she continued, plumbing every depth of her own misery. "To be your queen and give you heirs. You will marry her, give her plump-cheeked, blue-eyed babies, and the whole country will rejoice."

He jerked his head back to look at her, and his blue eyes seemed to glitter in the moonlight.

"Yes, Jasmine. Is that what you want to hear? Yes. I must take a royal virgin to be my queen. She will give me heirs. It is required of me as king. The Al'Ramiz lineage goes back a thousand years. I must have children of my own bloodline. I *will* have them. Does that satisfy you?"

Her heart pounded painfully in her throat.

"Yes," she choked out. "It's exactly what I wanted to hear."

Exactly what she needed: the finally crushing blow to any glimmer of hope. The brief illusion of being young again, of going back to the time they were in love, was gone.

Kareef wasn't hers anymore. Married or not, he had never truly been hers.

A night breeze cut through the courtyard, causing her hair to whip darkly across her face. She heard the plaintive call of owls in the shadowy darkness. The spice and warmth of the air whirled around Jasmine. The memory of his touch a moment ago still burned her cheek.

She heard servants calling his name, louder this time. Any moment now, the servants would find them.

With a deep breath, Kareef stepped toward her.

"But the day of my marriage is far away," he said, tucking her hair gently behind her ear. "And we will take the time we have. Tomorrow, I will take you to the desert."

She shivered at his touch. "And there you will divorce me?"

He smiled, and the dark hunger in his eyes made her tremble. "Good night, my jewel." Lowering his head, he kissed her cheek. "Until tomorrow."

"Yes," she whispered, pulling away. As the servants found Kareef, exclaiming excitedly that his brother, Tahir, had been found, she hurried back to her tiny room in the servants' wing. She ran until she was out of breath.

But even as she collapsed on her small bed, she could still feel Kareef behind her, still feel his lips on hers.

She knew what awaited her tomorrow. She knew it by the dark hunger she'd seen in his eyes. He meant to take her in the desert. *To take her in his bed.*

No! She would not—would *not*—surrender!

CHAPTER FOUR

IT WAS high noon the next day when Kareef arrived at Qusay International Airport.

He'd spent the whole morning in meetings with advisers and undersecretaries, signing papers and discussing upcoming treaties. But he'd smiled all morning. He couldn't stop anticipating the pleasure that was to come.

Tonight, he would finally have Jasmine in his bed.

Kissing her last night had been incredible. If his servants hadn't come out into the garden to find him—something he could not fault them for, since he'd ordered them to tell him if they ever got his youngest brother, Tahir, on the phone—Kareef would have thrown Jasmine over his shoulder and taken her straight to the royal bedchamber.

But this way would be much better. They would have privacy in Qais. And if there was one thing he hungered for almost as much as Jasmine in his bed, it was the freedom of the desert.

Jasmine was right. Their paths lay elsewhere. He would allow her to follow the path she'd chosen for herself. He would give Jasmine her divorce.

But not yet.

For now, Kareef had only one desire. One need. To satisfy this all-consuming hunger of thirteen years.

For her.

Was she sleeping now in that little bed of hers in the palace? Was she naked? Was she dreaming? He closed his eyes, imagining her hair tousled, her soft body warm beneath the blankets. He growled. Every moment away from her seemed wasted.

But at least this particular royal appointment was one he'd looked forward to. As his chauffeur opened the door of the silver limousine, Kareef climbed out, the wind whirling his ceremonial white robes around his ankles as he glanced around him on the tarmac.

Behind him was the second limousine of his motorcade; to the left were four uniformed motorcyclists and his own Bentley, with flags bearing the royal insignia of Qusay whipping in the wind. Directly in front of him he saw his brother's Gulfstream jet, newly arrived from Australia.

His spirits rose still higher.

A perfect day, he thought. Jasmine would soon be in his bed. Rafiq had just returned to Qusay, and even Tahir, who'd been in self-imposed exile for so many years, was on the way. Kareef's heart suddenly felt as bright as the Qusani sun shimmering heat against his white robes.

Rafiq appeared at the door of his airplane. At thirty, there were faint lines at his brother's narrowed eyes, a ruthless set of his jaw that hadn't been there before. Years building a worldwide business empire had changed Rafiq every bit as much as Kareef's years in the desert had changed him.

But as his brother came down the steps to the tarmac, looking every inch the sleek, sharp tycoon in his gray Armani suit, Kareef took one look at him and grinned. "Rafiq!"

"It is good to see you, big brother," Rafiq replied, taking Kareef by the arm. Pulling him close, he slapped him on the back, then teased, "Or should I call you 'sire'?"

With a snort, Kareef waved the joke aside. He ushered his brother into the cool interior of the waiting limousine and the chauffeur closed the door solidly behind them. The motorcade pulled away, motorcycle lights flashing as they left the airport. "It's good you could come at such short notice."

"You think I would miss your coronation?"

"You almost missed Xavian's wedding. How long were you here? Three? Four hours at most."

"It is true," Rafiq conceded. "Although as it turns out, he wasn't Xavian, our cousin after all. But there was no way I was not coming for your coronation. And if there is one thing I am sure of, Kareef, it's that you are indeed my brother." They exchanged a grin, their eyes the same shade of blue, each with the same chiselled jawline. "Speaking of brothers, where is Tahir? Is our wayward brother to grace us with his presence this time?"

Kareef frowned. "I spoke with him…." Name of God, was it only last night, after he'd left Jasmine in the garden? It seemed far longer than that. He'd spent all night dreaming of Jasmine—and all morning dealing with Akmal, his vizier, who was furious at Kareef's plans to leave for the desert. He smiled broadly. "I spoke with him yesterday."

"I don't believe it!"

"It's true. Though it wasn't easy to track him down in Monte Carlo, he's coming to the coronation."

"All three of us, back here at the same time?" his brother said in amazement.

"It's been too long," Kareef agreed.

Rafiq suddenly gave him a sharp look. "That's quite a smile."

He blinked. "Of course I would smile. You're here and Tahir is on his way."

His brother narrowed his eyes, looking at him keenly. "You're smiling with your whole face," he observed. "I haven't seen you do that for years. Care to explain?"

"You'll know everything soon enough." And he feared it was true. Rafiq had always been the sharpest—the most ruthless—of the brothers. To change the subject, Kareef leaned forward and slapped his hands on his thighs. "But you are here and that, my brother, is a good thing. I hear your business goes from strength to strength. Tell me more."

The journey through the city was swift as traffic halted for the king's motorcade. Kareef tried to pay attention to the details of the new emporiums Rafiq had just opened in Auckland and Perth, but his mind kept wandering to the woman who waited for him at the palace. And the night that awaited them in the desert.

Jasmine would resist him. He knew that. He also knew she would fall. She would be in his bed—tonight. Tomorrow. And the day after that, if he still wanted her. He would make love to her until they were both utterly spent.

Then, and only then he would speak the words that would part them forever. And let her go on to her marriage.

His smile faltered. The motorcade went past the palace gate and stopped beneath a portico. A turbaned footman opened his door. As they went up the sweeping steps, Kareef glanced back at his brother. Rafiq seemed dazed as he stared up at the turrets and domes reaching into the sky, glowing like a pearl beneath the noonday sun.

Kareef stopped, taking his brother by the arm. "Here I must leave you, my brother. So if you will excuse me…"

Rafiq cocked a suspicious eyebrow. "Off to place a bet on the Qais Cup?"

Kareef laughed. "I haven't gambled on a horse race in years."

"Then it's being crowned king," he guessed. "All that raw power." He winked. "I'm almost envious, my brother."

"No." That definitely wasn't it. "Excuse me."

"Then what is it?" his brother called after him. "What's got you so damned *happy*?"

Kareef didn't answer. He hurried down the stone cloister of ancient Byzantine arches around the courtyard. Servants stopped to bow as he rushed past them, his white robes whipping around his ankles. In the courtyard, the sun shone bright and hot. A warm breeze blew through the palm trees, rich with the fragrance of spice and oranges.

Her scent.

He glanced at the bright blue sky, hearing birdsong

from the garden. It was after noon, and he hadn't yet eaten. But he hungered for only one thing.

He found Jasmine waiting in her small bedroom in the servants' wing, sitting on the bed reading a paperback book, her packed suitcase at her feet. When he opened the door, she looked up, her expression grave and pale.

"Finally, I am ready." He glanced around the tiny, shabby room, noticing it for the first time. He cleared his throat. "I regret this was the only room available in the palace…."

"That's quite all right," she said quietly, marking her place and tucking her book in her suitcase. "This room has suited me very well." She rose to her feet. "Shall we go?"

Her wide eyes looked up at him, the color of sepia fringed in black. She was wearing a short modern dress in pink silk. Her dark hair was pulled back in a chignon beneath a little felt hat. Her look was retro, modern and with a quirky style all her own.

She looked sixteen still. The same pale, olive-hued skin. The same full black lashes, sweeping over high cheekbones. The same full, luscious lips, bare of makeup. The color of roses.

He longed to kiss those lips.

He was already hard for her.

No wonder. He'd been celibate for… He didn't like to think about that. He'd thought he was too busy for women, or simply uninterested in the particular succession of gold diggers who threw themselves at royalty on a daily basis, even if he had been only minor royalty until recently.

Now he knew the truth. His body had hungered for only one woman. The woman in front of him now.

He could hardly wait to satiate himself with her. It was a journey of several hours to the desert. His eyes fell upon her tiny bed. He was not sure he could wait that long….

But even as he considered the size of her bed, she'd already left the room, dragging her tiny suitcase behind her. He caught up with her, lifting up the suitcase on his shoulder.

"Thank you," she said gravely.

"It weighs almost nothing." And it truly did. He carried it easily with one hand. "Why did you pack so little?"

"Um." Her lips turned upward at the corners. "To avoid baggage fees at the airport?"

He snorted a laugh. "Hajjar has his own plane." He shook his head. "You always enjoyed dress-up as a girl, always had your own style different from the rest." He smiled. "Has so much changed for you? You're too busy to worry about clothes, now that you run your own multimillion dollar company in New York?"

"Ah. Well." Her eyes shifted away uneasily. "Umar has already picked out the clothes he thinks appropriate for me. They will arrive from Paris in a few days. So he didn't—I mean, *I* didn't—see much point in bringing my own clothes from New York, especially since we'll only be in Qusay until we're married."

"I see." He was suddenly irritated by the thought of anyone telling Jasmine what to wear. He tried to shrug it off. If Jasmine didn't care, why should he? Her relationship with Umar was none of his business. In fact,

Kareef was determined to make them both forget his existence for the next few days.

Outside the palace, a bodyguard hefted the small suitcase from Kareef and carried it to the bottom of the sweeping stairs. Another assistant packed it in the front SUV of the motorcade.

Jasmine looked at the SUV and limousine behind it, and all the many bodyguards and servants bustling around the motorcade, with palpable relief. "I see we're not traveling alone."

"Don't get too excited. I travel as the king of Qusay." He gave her a sudden wicked grin. "But in the desert, that will change. As you said, in the desert I'll be just a man. Like any other…"

He let his voice trail off suggestively and saw her shiver in the sunlight. As his chauffeur opened the door, she was very careful not to touch Kareef as she scooted past him into the backseat of the Rolls-Royce.

Sitting beside her, Kareef leaned back, glancing at her out of the corner of his eye as the motorcade drove out the palace gate. She was clinging to the farthest side of the car. It almost amused him. Did she really think she would get out of this without falling into his bed?

Well, let her continue to think so. He loved nothing more than a challenge.

And she had nothing to feel guilty about. Not in this case. Nor in the other—

Memory trembled on the edge of his consciousness, threatening to darken his sunshine. He pushed the troubling memory away. He wouldn't think of what they'd lost in the past—what he'd caused her to lose. Today would be about one thing only: pleasure.

The motorcade moved swiftly out of the city, heading northeast along the coast. But with Jasmine sitting against the opposite window, doing her level best not to touch him, every mile seemed to stretch out to eternity.

He should have listened to Akmal Al'Sayr, he thought grimly. His vizier had tried to convince him to use one of his royal helicopters or planes currently shuttling foreign dignitaries to Qusay, rather than waste time traveling by car. Now Kareef wished he'd taken that advice. Coddling diplomats suddenly seemed a much lower priority than getting Jasmine into his bed.

Kareef glanced at her. She refused to look in his direction, continuing instead to stare stonily out the darkly tinted window. Behind her, he could see the bright turquoise sea shining beyond the smooth, modern highway.

Neither of them moved, but tension hummed between them.

He wanted her. Wanted to take her right here and now in the backseat of this limousine. But was that the private, discreet affair he wanted? Tossing her like a whore in the backseat of a Rolls-Royce, with bodyguards surely able to guess what went on behind darkened windows?

Kareef cursed beneath his breath. He would just have to wait.

But as they approached a fork in the road, he suddenly leaned forward.

"Turn here," he ordered.

"Sire?" His chauffeur looked back in surprise.

"Take the old desert road," he commanded in a voice that did not brook opposition. As his bodyguard communicated the order over a walkie-talkie to the SUV in front of the motorcade, his chauffeur switched lanes on the modern highway, heading toward the exit that would lead straight north through the sands and rock, toward the desert of Qais.

He sat back. He might have to be patient, but he'd be damned if he wouldn't get it over with as soon as possible, by taking the most direct route.

The modern highway of Qusay stretched around the circumference of the island, a new way to travel north to the principality of Qais, a harsh landscape of desert sands and cragged, desolate mountains. Only two years ago, Kareef, as Prince of Qais, had finished the highway with the new influx of money brought by his developments, including the blossoming sport of horse racing. Qais was now second only to Dubai as the emerging hotspot on the thoroughbred racing circuit.

Ironic, Kareef thought, that after personally giving up the sport, the thing he'd once loved the most in the world, he'd turned it into a thriving industry for others.

Although that wasn't entirely true. There had once been something he'd loved even more than horse racing.

He glanced at Jasmine. Her beautiful face was wan. Dark circles were beneath her eyes, hollows beneath her cheeks.

Damn it all to hell.

Why was she trying to resist what they both wanted?

He turned back to the window. Rolling dunes sifted scattered sand onto the road, brushed by wind beneath the hot sun. The road was very old, dating to his grandfather's time. During sandstorms this road could disappear altogether.

Disappear. As he'd tried to do thirteen years ago.

He'd wanted to die rather than face the accusation in her eyes. He'd fled into the desert, praying to be sucked beneath a grave of sand.

Instead, Umar Hajjar had found him and brought him home. Unable to die, Kareef had thrown himself into a life of sacrifice and duty. The nomadic people of the desert had eventually looked to him for leadership, turning his family's honorary title of Prince of Qais into a real one.

Against his will, Kareef had been brutally sentenced—to live.

He rubbed the back of his tense neck, giving Jasmine a sideways glance. He would never be able to make amends to her for what he'd done.

But should he try?

He wanted her. But did that mean he had the right to take her? Should he try to do one last unselfish thing…by letting her go?

One man has had no trouble resisting me, Kareef. You.

He suppressed a harsh laugh. He, who'd shown such perfect control with women, lost all self-control around her. Prickles of heat went through his body just sitting beside her.

Any man would be attracted to Jasmine. Even if he were blind. Even if she were wrapped in veils from head to toe. Any man would seek her warmth. Her scent, a tantalizing mix of citrus and clove. Her seductive shape, with that tiny waist setting off her delectable breasts and the wide curve of her hips. The perfect backside for any man's hands. The heartbreaking sweetness of her glance. Of her soul.

No, he would not think of her soul. He would think only of her body.

"We're not going to stop, are we?" she suddenly whispered. Her voice sounded tortured. "We're not going to stop on the way?"

He turned to her. Her beautiful brown eyes were shimmering with light.

"Do you wish to stop?" he asked in a low voice.

She shook her head. "I want to drive through the mountains as quickly as possible."

"Are you afraid?"

This time, she had no bravado in her.

"Yes," she whispered. "You know what I fear. I see it in my nightmares. Don't you?"

Kareef's throat closed. He gave a single unsteady nod.

Here on the old desert road, they would drive right past the riding school and the red rock mountains beyond. The cliffs. The hidden cave. The place where he hadn't protected her, where he hadn't protected the child neither of them had known she was carrying. Where Jasmine had nearly died of fever because he'd given the ridiculous promise not to tell after the horse-riding accident. As if love alone could save them.

He'd been helpless. Useless. He'd failed at the most basic test of any man. Jagged pain cracked his throat, making his voice husky as he said, "We will not stop."

He saw her take a deep, grateful breath. "Thank you."

He nodded, not trusting himself to speak. Long ago, they'd escaped the prying eyes of the palace at the riding school. Her friend Sera had distracted the girls' aged chaperone so Kareef and Jasmine could have some precious time together—alone.

The remote school, surrounded by paddocks and stables, had been where Kareef felt most truly alive, the place he'd loved to race his black stallion, Razul. He'd loved to feel Jasmine's eyes on him as he showed off for her.

"Ride with me, Jasmine," he'd begged, adding with a grin, *"You're not afraid, are you?"* And one day— she'd finally agreed.

They'd thought themselves so clever, to evade the restrictions set by her parents and find a way to be together. But in the end, fate had punished them all— even her strict but well-meaning parents whose only crime had been trying to protect Jasmine from a man who might bring destruction and shame to her loving, innocent soul and fairy-tale beauty. *A man like him.*

As their motorcade traveled through the desert, he stared out at the sharp light of the sun reflecting against the sand. Scattered clouds like yin and yang symbols of darkness and light moved swiftly against the bright blue sky. He wondered if a storm was coming.

Then he felt her small hand on his arm and knew the storm was already here. Inside him.

"Thank you," Jasmine whispered again. Her fingers tightened on his arm. "Umar is a kind man, he tries to be good to me, but I did not wish to face this for the first time beside him, traveling through the desert on my wedding day." She shook her head, lifting her luminous eyes to his. "He can't understand. You do."

At the light touch of her fingers, he shuddered.

If he were a civilized man, he thought suddenly,

he'd set her free right now. He would divorce her immediately and let her go untouched to the man she wished to marry. His friend. But the thought of her with any other man was as sharp as a razor blade inside him.

Kareef wanted her for himself.

Wanted? Was that even close to the right word? His body craved her, like it craved food or water or air.

Wanted?

He wanted her so much that she made his body shake with need. It was an inhuman test of will that he should be so close to her, trapped in the back of a Rolls-Royce but unable to touch her.

With a shuddering intake of breath, he looked down at her hand on his arm, fighting to control himself when all he wanted to do was seize her in his arms and crush her lips against his own.

But after all his time living unselfishly to serve others, could he really allow himself to take what he needed, what he wanted most?

What would it cost her if he did?

Kareef heard the intake of Jasmine's breath, felt her body move against his, and he knew she'd just seen the riding school on the other side of the road. He put his arm around her. He felt her body tremble. She stared out at the school as they passed, her face stricken, her brown eyes swimming with tears like an ocean of memories.

And in that instant he forgot about his own needs.

He forgot the heat of his own desire.

All he knew was that it was Jasmine in his arms, Jasmine who was afraid—and that he had to protect her. Holding her against his chest, he leaned forward urgently and barked out an order to his chauffeur. "Drive faster."

The man nodded and pressed on the gas.

The riding school passed by in a blur of color. He saw the place where they'd first whispered words of love. The place where he'd drawn her into a quiet glade of trees behind the farthest paddock, and on a soft blanket beside a cool brook—the place he'd first made love to her, virgins both, pledging hushed, breathless, eternal devotion.

"I marry you," she'd whispered three times.

"I marry you," he'd answered once, holding her hands tightly between his own.

Kareef took a deep breath.

He would be unselfish—one last time.

In the old days, the king's will in Qusay had been absolute. No one could deny the king the woman he wanted, under pain of death. He would have taken possession of Jasmine like a barbarian. He would have thrown her into his harem, locked the door behind them and not come out again until he was satisfied. He would have taken her on a bed, against a wall, on the soft carpets in front of the fire. He would have lifted her against him, the firelight gleaming off the sweat of her silken skin, until he made her gasp and scream his name.

But Kareef was not that barbarian king. He couldn't be. Not when Jasmine trembled with fear in his arms.

"The memories can't hurt us anymore," he murmured, holding her tight as he stroked her hair. "It all happened long ago."

"I know that. In my mind," she whispered, her voice barely loud enough to hear. "But in my heart, it happened yesterday."

They stared out the window as the motorcade flew past the humble outbuildings of the riding school, its paddocks and fields and stables.

The intimacy of being so physically close as they shared the same exact memories made him taut with an emotion he didn't want to feel. His muscles shook from the effort of just holding her, of just offering comfort—thirteen years too late.

Then they were past it. The school disappeared behind them. Their limousine flew down the bumpy old road through the red rock canyon toward Qais.

He felt Jasmine relax in his arms. Closing his eyes, he breathed in the scent of her hair. She leaned against his chest. For long moments of silence, he held her. Just the two of them. Like long ago.

Then Kareef heard the cough of his bodyguard in the front seat, heard his chauffeur shift position. And he forced himself to pull away from their compromising position.

He looked down at her, gently lifting her chin.

"You're all right then?" he said softly, offering her a smile.

Her eyes shone back at him with unshed tears.

"I was wrong," she whispered. Her dark eyelashes trembled against her pale cheeks. "I see that now. I was wrong to hate you," she said softly, reaching out to hold his hand. "Thank you for holding me. I couldn't have faced that alone."

He stared at her incredulously.

She was forgiving him? For one brief moment of sympathy, the kind any stranger might have offered to a grieving woman, she was willing to overlook what he'd done?

He looked away, his jaw tense. "Forget it."

"But you—"

"It was nothing," he bit out, ripping his hand from her grasp.

He would let her go, he told himself fiercely. His only way of making amends. Honor and duty were all he had left. He would not seduce her. He wouldn't even touch her. As soon as they arrived at his home, he would immediately divorce her and send her on her way. He would leave her to her happiness.

His jaw clenched as he stared out at the sun.

For thirteen years, he'd buried himself so deeply in duty that he couldn't breathe or think. He'd immolated himself like some mad desert hermit buried neck-deep in hot sand. But being near Jasmine had brought his body and soul alive in a way he hadn't felt in a long time. In a way he'd never thought he'd feel again.

But he would let her go. No matter how he wanted her. *He owed her.* He would let her disappear from his life, and this time it would be forever. Umar Hajjar would guard her covetously, like the treasure she was.

Kareef would be unselfish one last time. Even if it killed him. He almost hoped it would.

The shadows of the red rock mountains moved in mottled patterns over their motorcade as they passed out of the canyon. As they went through the mountains into the wide sweep of the desert of Qais, he saw the wind picking up, swirling little spirals of sand, twisting them up into the sky.

Kareef felt the same way every time he looked at her. Tangled up in her.

He felt her dark head nestle on his shoulder. Looking down at her in surprise, he saw her eyes were closed. She was sleeping against him. His gaze roamed her face.

God, he wanted to kiss her.

More than kiss. He wanted to strip her naked and feast on every inch of her supple flesh. He wanted to explore the mountains of her breasts and valley between. The low flat plain of her belly and hot citadel between her thighs. He wanted to devour her like a conqueror seizing a kingdom for his own use, beneath his hands, beneath his control.

But the old days were over.

He was king of Qusay, yet unable to have the one thing he most desired. No strength could take her. No brutality could force her. He couldn't act on his desire. Not at the expense of her happiness.

His muscles hurt with the effort it took to feel her against him, but not touch her. Clenching his jaw, he turned back out the window. He could see his house in the distance. In just a few minutes, they would be done. He would go inside, find the emerald and speak the simple words to set her free. And after today, he would make sure he never saw Jasmine again—

His thoughts were interrupted when he heard a sudden squeal, the sickening sound of metal grating against the road.

As if in a dream, he looked up to see the SUV at the

front of the motorcade slam hard to the right, then smash against the rock wall along the road.

He heard his own bodyguard shout, saw his chauffeur frantically try to turn the wheel. But it was too late. Kareef barely had time to think before he felt the Rolls-Royce hit against the SUV, felt his body jack-knife forward.

As their limousine flew up, rolling violently through the air, he looked down at Jasmine. His last image was her wide-open, terrified eyes—his last sound, her scream.

CHAPTER FIVE

JASMINE opened her eyes.

She was lying on a blanket, amid the cool shadows of green trees. Nearby, she heard a burbling brook and horses racing in the paddocks of the riding school. She felt the soft desert wind against her face. And the greatest miracle of all: the boy she loved was beside her, smiling with his whole face, love shining from his electric blue eyes.

He pulled her down against him on the blanket, reaching to tuck her hair behind her ear. Dappled golden light caressed his black hair as he rolled over her body with sudden urgency, his eyes gazing fiercely down into hers.

"I have no right to ask you this," he whispered. "But I will regret it forever if I do not." He cupped her face in his hands. "Marry me, Jasmine. Marry me."

"Yes," she gasped. He smiled, then with agonizing slowness he lowered his lips toward hers. He kissed her. Then, for the first time, they did far more than just kiss....

"Jasmine!"

His sudden harsh shout was jarring. She heard the

panic in his voice, but couldn't answer. Something was choking her. Slowly, blearily she opened her eyes.

And realized she wasn't on the blanket by the stream.

She was strapped into a car upside down. Her knees were hanging against her chest and she could see the blue sky through the window at her feet. The seat belt felt so tight that she couldn't breathe. Something warm and liquid dripped across her lashes.

"I'm bleeding," she whispered aloud.

She heard Kareef's curse and suddenly the passenger door was wrenched open, causing scattered pieces of broken glass to clatter from the window to the road. Suddenly, the seat belt was gone and she was in Kareef's arms, sitting on his knees in the dusty road.

She felt his hands move over her head, her arms, her body. "Nothing's broken," he breathed. He held her tightly against his chest, kissing her hair, whispering, "You're safe. You're safe."

She closed her eyes in the shelter of his arms. She pressed her cheek against the warmth of his neck.

Time felt as mixed and confused as the smashed, upside-down cars in the road. For the space of a dream, she'd been sixteen again, with her whole life ahead of her, certain of Kareef's devotion and his strong arms around her.

Those same arms were around her now, even more powerful and muscled than they'd been before. What had happened?

"Get a doctor!" Kareef turned and thundered.

She was dimly aware of bodyguards rushing around them, shouting into cell phones, but they all seemed far away. She and Kareef were at the eye of the storm.

She looked at him and saw the blood on his clothes, the tears in the white fabric of his shirt, and a chill went through her. Trembling, she reached her hand toward his face, toward the thin lines of red streaking his chiseled cheekbone. "You're bleeding."

He jerked his head away. "It's nothing."

He didn't want her to touch him. That much was absolutely clear. She felt her cheeks go hot as she put her hand down. She pressed her lips together, wanting to cry. So much had changed since the time of her beautiful dream. "But—you should see a doctor."

He rose to his feet, holding her. "Unnecessary. But for you..." He looked down at Jasmine. "Can you stand alone?"

"Yes." Her head was pounding, but she would not try to lean against him. She would not make him push her away. If he did not want her to touch him, she would stand alone on her own two feet if it killed her.

Releasing her hand, he brushed dirt off the shoulders of her pink blouson minidress. "Your hat is gone," he muttered.

She looked up at him in a daze. "It doesn't matter."

"We'll have someone find it." Taking a damp towel from a bodyguard, Kareef wiped her forehead, then paused. "You've got a small cut on your scalp," he said matter-of-factly, his voice calm, as if trying not to scare her. He turned back to his bodyguard. "We must take Miss Kouri back to the hospital."

Miss Kouri. So he'd reverted to that. He was already keeping his distance, as if he'd already divorced her.

The bodyguard shook his head at Kareef. "The cars

are totaled, your highness." His voice grew bitter, angry. "That mare escaped into the road again. Youssef had to swerve to avoid her."

Kareef looked past the smashed, upside-down Rolls-Royce toward the black horse still standing in the road. "Ah, Bara'ah. Even put out to pasture," he murmured softly, "you're up to your old tricks."

Jasmine followed his gaze. The slender black mare, chewing lone wisps of grass that had grown through the cracks of the pavement, looked back with placid amusement.

"Get her back in her paddock," Kareef said. "Get a new car from my garage."

His garage?

Jasmine looked down the road and saw a wide, low-slung ranch house of brown wood, surrounded by paddocks and palm trees.

Comfortable and peaceful, without any of Umar's gilded, lavish ostentatiousness, Kareef's home was a green oasis in the vast wasteland of the desert.

He'd done it. He'd created the house he'd once promised her. But he'd done it alone....

Her hands tightened. And Kareef wanted to take her away. He wanted to take her back to the city, to leave her in some sterile, beeping hospital room—alone. Perhaps he intended to run inside and get the emerald, and divorce her on the way?

It was what she'd thought she wanted—a quick divorce without seduction, without entanglements. But now, she suddenly felt like crying.

"I don't want to go to the hospital."

At the sound of her voice, Kareef and the bodyguard turned to her in surprise, as if they'd forgotten she was there.

"But Jasmine," Kareef replied gently and slowly, as if speaking to a recalcitrant child, "you need to see a doctor."

"No hospital." Dark hair blew in her eyes from her collapsing chignon. Pushing back her hair, she saw blood on her hands. Looking down, she saw drops of blood on the pink silk of her dress.

Just like the last time she'd been in an accident. The last time she'd seen her own blood. After the accident—before the scandal…

She suddenly couldn't get enough air.

She couldn't breathe.

Panicking, she put her hands on her head as she tried to get air in her lungs. More dark tendrils tumbled from her chignon as the world started to spin around her.

Kareef's eyes narrowed. "Jasmine?"

Her breath came in short, shallow gasps as she backed away from him. Everything was a blur, going in circles faster and faster. No matter which way she looked, she saw something that trapped her. The home of her dreams. The man of her dreams. The blood on her dress…

Kareef grabbed her before she could fall. His intense blue eyes stared down at her. She dimly heard him shouting. She saw his men rushing to obey.

She saw Kareef's lips moving, saw the concern in his blue eyes, but couldn't hear what he was saying. She could only hear the ragged pant of her own breathing, the frantic pounding of her own heart.

Colors continued to spin around her as her knees started to slide. In the distance she saw the black mare staring back at her. Black like the horse who'd thrown her long ago. Black like the accident that had caused her to lose everything.

Black.

Black.

Black…

Suddenly, Kareef's worried face came into sharp focus.

"You're awake," he said in a low voice. "Do you know who I am?"

Jasmine discovered that she was lying on her back in a bedroom she didn't recognize. Her head was pounding; her throat was dry.

She tried to sit up. "Where—where am I?"

"Don't try to move," he said, pushing her back gently on the bed. "My own doctor's on the way."

Her head was flat on the pillow as she looked slowly around the bedroom. It was large, rustic and comfortable, with a king-sized bed and spartan furnishings. It was very masculine, smelling of leather and wood. She looked at the small fireplace made out of hewn rock. "I'm in your bedroom?"

"So you know who I am," Kareef said, sounding relieved.

Jasmine gave a derisive snort. "The illustrious king of Qusay, the adored and revered prince of Qais, the delight of all harem girls everywhere, the…"

"How hard did that glass hit your head?" he demanded, but his mouth quirked up into a smile. He'd been worried, she realized. Very worried.

"Did I faint?" She tried to sit up, to show them both she was all right.

"Don't move!"

"I feel fine!"

"The doctor will be the judge of that."

"You said I have a small cut on my scalp. That doesn't require a team of specialists. Stick a bandage on my head."

"And you fainted," he reminded her.

Her cheeks went hot with embarrassment. She felt sure her fainting had nothing to do with the bump on her head and had been instead some kind of panic attack—but how could she explain that without bringing up the long-ago accident she absolutely, positively did not want to talk about?

She didn't need to bring it up. His next words proved that.

"What is it about you and doctors?" he said softly, looking down at her. "Why do you refuse to let me take decent care of you?"

Their eyes locked, and she sucked in her breath. She knew what he was thinking about.

After the horse-riding accident, he'd pleaded to fetch a doctor. But she'd refused. She been desperate to keep her shame a secret, to protect her family. *Please, Kareef, just hold me, I'll be fine,* she'd cried. But when she'd started shaking with fever, he'd broken his word. He'd returned with a doctor and two servants he thought he could trust.

One of the servants had been Marwan, who'd betrayed them the instant Kareef disappeared into the desert. Her family had been devastated, nearly destroyed. *Because of her.*

Blinking fast, she turned her head away.

Kareef leaned over the bed. With the prison of his arms on the mattress around her, she slowly looked up into his face.

Their faces was inches apart. Tension coiled between them.

"Here," he muttered, looking away. "Let me fix this."

He reached behind her and rearranged the pillows. He lifted her, and she closed her eyes, relishing the warmth and strength of his arms. Then he gently pushed her back against the pillows, into a sitting position. He stroked her hair.

"Better?" he said in a low voice.

His mouth was inches from her own. She felt the warmth of his breath against her skin. It made her shiver from her mouth to her earlobes to her nipples and neck. Even her supposedly injured scalp tingled with a feeling that had nothing to do with pain and everything to do with—

She cut off the thought. With Kareef so close to her, she was having difficulty thinking straight. What question had he asked her? She licked her lips. "I'm much…much better…."

"The doctor will be here soon," he said hoarsely. The hard muscles of his body seemed strained, almost shaking, as if he were struggling to hold himself in check. "Any moment, he will be here…."

He started to pull away. And suddenly Jasmine couldn't bear to lose his arms around her. Not after she'd been so cold for so long. Not when they were this close, this man she'd tried to hate, this man she'd never stopped craving.

Leaning up, she pressed her mouth to his.

It was a short kiss. A peck. Just enough to feel the roughness of his lips, his masculine power and strength. But it caused a hot fever to spread through her body.

Kareef looked down at her in shock. She heard his hoarse, ragged breath as his hands gripped her shoulders.

Then, with a growl, he pushed her back against the pillow as the simmering conflagration exploded into fire. He kissed her, hard and deep. His kiss was hungry. Brutal.

He kissed her as if he'd been starving for her half his life.

His arms wrapped around her, pressing Jasmine back against the pillows. He enfolded her small body with his larger one. His mouth was rough and savage against hers, bruising her lips even as his hands caressed the back of her head, holding her like a fragile rose.

The hot demand of his kiss seared her, sending sparks down her body. Her breasts felt heavy, her nipples tightening to painful intensity. An ache of longing coiled low in her belly, curling lower, lower still, between her thighs.

His mouth never left hers as he stroked down the front of her body, from the smooth curve of her collarbone to her flat belly, seeing her with his fingertips. His feather-light touch against the smooth pink silk of her blouson dress caused exquisite agony of sensation. His kiss deepened, became more demanding. He gripped her bare arms, her shoulders, holding her down.

How many nights had she dreamed of this? Of feeling his hands on her skin, of being in his bed?

She was dreaming. She had to be. And she prayed she would never wake.

His large hands splayed across her silken belly in the bright sunlight of the windows. He plundered her lips, spreading her mouth wide to accept his tongue.

A soft moan escaped her. She wrapped her hands around his neck to hold his body against her. Their tongues intertwined, mingled, fought. His lips bruised hers—or was it the other way around? She no longer knew. Neither of them could hold thirteen years of desire in check. They barely kept themselves from causing injury to the other beneath the weight of their mutual, insatiable hunger.

It was better than it had been at sixteen. Now, at twenty-nine, she knew how rare this fire truly was.

She reached her hands beneath his shirt and felt the heat of his skin, the hard knots of his muscles and taut belly. Felt the soft coarse hair between the hard nubs of his nipples. With an intake of breath, he pulled back, grabbing her wrists.

"Tonight, you are mine. Whatever the cost." His voice was low and dark, as if ripped from the depths of his soul. "I will make you forget all the others."

Their eyes locked in a moment that seemed to stretch out to infinity. She swallowed.

"There have been no others," she whispered. "Only you. How could I give my body to another, when I am still your wife?"

Her cheeks went hot, and she couldn't meet his eyes. Would he mock her pathetic fidelity? Would he laugh at her?

Then she heard his harsh intake of breath. *"Jasmine."*

Suddenly, his hands were in her long tangled hair, his body pressed against hers. His blue eyes were dark and hungry as he tilted back her head, exposing her throat.

"Jasmine. My first," he breathed. "My only."

Her heartbeat tripled. Could he mean…?

No! It wasn't possible. He was a handsome, powerful sheikh, the king of Qusay. He couldn't have spent the last thirteen years as she had done—with a lonely bed and an aching heart!

But as Kareef's eyes burned through hers, she felt the truth. He stroked down her cheek, tracing his thumb against her bottom lip. Trembling, she closed her eyes as he touched her. This couldn't be happening…couldn't be…

Cupping her chin in his hands, he kissed her fiercely. His kiss was so deep and pure that she was reborn in the blaze, fired in the crucible of their desire. His hands moved beneath the pink dress, pressing rough and raw against her skin. He ripped the silk off her body, and she felt his hands everywhere. On the skin of her back as he undid her bra in a single swift movement. On her belly and hips as he pulled her white panties off, ripping them down over her long legs.

And suddenly, she was naked and spread across his bed.

Rising abruptly from the bed, he pinned her with his hot gaze as he slowly unbuttoned his tattered white shirt and cuffs. He dropped the shirt to the ground, then kicked off his black shoes and pants. From where she lay, naked on his white bedspread, she looked up at him and drew in her breath.

His tanned body was magnificent in the brilliant,

blinding sunlight from the windows, casting a halo over him like a dark angel. Shadows flickered over his well-built chest and downward, against a line of black hair that stretched past his taut belly to the thick length of him, so hard for her, jutted and proud in its unyielding, brutal masculine demand.

A cry caught in her throat as she looked at him. He knelt over her on the bed, his muscular thighs stretching over hers as he ran his broad hands down the length of her flat belly.

His fingers, once rough, became tantalizingly light. His fingertips barely made contact with her skin as he traced her hips and thighs. He cupped her breasts, feeling their weight, worshipping them. Kneeling over her, he kissed her neck, then her mouth.

He kissed her with reverence that seared her to the ends of her soul. His hands caressed her heavy, aching breasts and she closed her eyes. She nearly protested as his lips left hers. Then she felt him move down her body as he lowered his mouth to her breast. Feeling his lips suckle her aching nipple, his tongue swirling against her and his teeth creating a pleasure almost like pain, she gasped, arching her back.

Whatever it cost her, she didn't want him to stop.

His lips and tongue were pure fire against her skin as he tasted her, sucking and biting each breast until her breath came in short little gasps and she cried out. His hands cupped her, squeezing the full flesh with increasing intensity until her breasts lifted of their own accord to meet his mouth. She felt the warmth of the bright sun against her skin, heard her own gasps as if from a distance. His hard body moved against hers, and desire swept her up with the intensity of need, suspending her breathless in midair.

He kissed down the soft length of her belly, pressing her breasts together to lick the deep crevice between them.

She felt the coarse hair of his muscular thighs move against her legs as he moved farther down her body. She felt the hard jut of his erection press against her, demanding attention, jerking hard when it brushed briefly against her skin. But he didn't position himself between her legs. Instead, she felt his hands caress her hips, between her thighs.

With a growl, he spread her legs apart.

She squeezed her eyes shut, blocking out the light. If she opened her eyes and saw his head between her thighs, she feared she'd lose control.

His jawline was rough and scratchy against her tender skin. She felt the heat of his breath against her thighs as, stretching her wide with his fingers, he took a long, languorous taste of her.

She cried out, arching her back violently. The back of her head sank into the soft piles of pillows as she shook beneath the shocking, unendurable waves of bliss.

The pleasure, oh God, the pleasure! Tension twisted and coiled inside her, sending her higher with every sweep of his tongue, with every tiny curling flick of his tip against her wet body. Her chin tilted back higher as her eyes closed, almost rolling back in her head. Her breaths came in increasingly desperate pants as his powerful tongue worked against her, widely lapping one moment, the next moment swirling light circles against the painfully taut center of her longing.

Reaching up his hands to feel her breasts, he continued to lick her. His tongue was a wet, hard column of heat and he slowly thrust it inside her.

New trembling started deep inside Jasmine. She put her hands up against the headboard to brace herself. She felt dizzy, her body spinning out of control.

He thrust his tongue farther inside her, stroking her hard nub softly with his thumb. Then he moved his tongue upward to her most sensitive spot and suckled her there, swirling her with his tongue as he pushed a thick finger inside her.

Then two fingers. Then—three.

Oh God…. She couldn't take this, she couldn't…

Her body shook as if by an earthquake traveling hundreds of miles an hour. Harder, higher, faster… Her body and soul opened to him like cracks in the desert rock, letting in the sun and wind. She felt him move up her body to kiss her neck, positioning his hard, wide length between her thighs. His hands grasped her wrists against the headboard, holding her fast. Holding her down.

But she was already caught. She looked up at him above her.

No man had ever been so beautiful. His eyes were a brilliant blue, searing her with his need and hunger. His jawline was taut and dark with new stubble. Sharp cheekbones cast shadows on his Roman nose, below the black slash of his eyebrows. He was her dark angel. Her husband. Jasmine's heart rose to her throat.

His returning gaze whipped through her soul. Made her lose all sense of place and time. All sense of where she ended and he began. They were one.

Staring into her eyes, he slowly thrust himself inside her. Ruthlessly, he watched her face as he pushed himself to the hilt, right to her heart.

She gasped at the feeling of him inside her. The size of him hurt her. Pleasure and pain together rolled over her body in waves before she stretched to accommodate him.

He drew back and pushed inside her again, so hard and deep—with such force—that another new wave of pleasure hit her, knocking her over and sucking her beneath the waves. Slowly, he rode her, pushing deeper with each thrust, until the pleasure was too much, too much, beyond thought or reason.

Gripping his shoulders in her hands, she cried out, exploding like a fire scattering embers in the night. And as she shattered into a million pieces like stars across the sky, she dimly heard her voice gasping his name, crying words of love as she fell.

CHAPTER SIX

WHEN Kareef heard her gasp with joy, when he felt her tremble and shake around him, it was almost too much. His first thrust was nearly his last.

But he was no longer an eighteen-year-old boy. He took a slow, shuddering breath, holding back his raging desire, regaining control. He held himself in ferocious check as he pushed inside her. It took every bit of will that he possessed to hold himself back.

It was bliss.

It was hell.

It was everything he'd dreamed and more.

He looked down and saw Jasmine's luscious body spread out beneath him, saw the afternoon sunlight against her full breasts, casting her pink, taut nipples in a warm glow as she arched her back. Her beautiful face was lost in an expression of fierce, agonized joy as he rode her. She triumphed in her possession of him, as he gloried in taking her.

The bright desert sunlight touched everywhere on her skin, like curling fingers. Her image washed over him like a wave of cool water. How long had he desired her? How long had he thirsted, like a perishing man for an oasis? How long had dreams of Jasmine Kouri tormented him, body and soul?

His hands shook as he gripped her shoulders, fighting to hold himself back from the thrust that would make him pour his seed into her.

He was no selfish boy, to take her quickly at his own pleasure. He would make it last. He'd brought her to fulfillment several times but it still wasn't enough. He wanted to give her more—to make her feel more. He wanted to make love to her all day, all night until she could bear no more.

"Jasmine," he whispered. His voice was raw even to his own ears.

He heard her soft, kittenish gasp in reply.

God, she was beautiful. He stared down into her face. The beautiful, beautiful face of the only woman he'd ever desired.

Lowering his head, he kissed her. She twisted beneath him, reaching her arms around his back, holding him down against her. He tightened in sweet agony.

Jasmine. He whispered her name soundlessly as he stroked up her naked body to her soft cheek. She was his, only his. There'd been no other lovers in her bed. He was the only man who'd ever possessed her.

The thought caused a surge to rush through his blood. Beads of sweat broke out on his forehead from the effort it took to hold back his own climax.

There was no need to hurry, he told himself. No need to rush. He had all the time in the world.

Pulling back, he slowly moved inside her. She

arched her back with a gasp, whispering rapturous words he could not hear.

With iron self-control, he thrust inside her again, riding her with increasing depth and speed. Their bodies became sweaty, sliding against each other as he pushed inside her with increasing roughness and force, almost impaling her as his muscled chest slid against the soft bounce of her breasts.

He couldn't hold back much longer...couldn't—

He felt her start to tighten again around him. Saw her hold her breath, then gasp, slowly letting out the air in a hiss through her full, reddened, bruised lips.

Suddenly, her nails gripped into his naked back. Screaming incomprehensible words, she twisted her hips, thrashing back and forth beneath him and he could hold back no longer. She screamed out his name, and he finally lost all control.

With a groan, he thrust inside her so deeply that almost at once, the orgasm hit him like a blow, with joy so intense he blacked out for several seconds.

It could have been minutes or hours later when he finally resurfaced. Kareef found himself naked on the bed, still holding her to his chest, with a sheet twisted haphazardly around them.

His heartbeat still hadn't returned to normal as he looked down at her beautiful, exhausted face. Tenderly, he bent his head to kiss her dirty, smudged forehead.

Her eyelashes fluttered open, and she looked up at him without speaking. He heard the ragged pant of her breath. For a moment, he just cradled her in his arms and they looked at each other silently in the roseate glow of twilight.

Then he heard a knock, heard the door push open.

"Sire, forgive me, I was assisting at a difficult labor, but now I'm ready to see the— Oh."

His trusted personal doctor, an elderly Qusani who'd been loyal to the Al'Ramiz family for genera-tions, had peeked his head around the door, and clearly he'd had a shock. The physician's cheeks burned red as he backed away. "Er—I'll wait outside 'til you're ready, and until then, leave the patient in your… er…capable hands."

The man left, discreetly closing the door behind him.

Kareef and Jasmine looked at each other, still naked and sprawled across the bed, with only the twisted sheet like a rope over them.

And to his surprise, she burst into laughter.

"So much for discretion," she said, wiping her eyes.

Kareef's eyes couldn't look away from her face as she laughed. Her sparkling eyes, her white teeth, the sound of her laugh. "He will never tell," he promised. But he couldn't stop smiling at her.

He'd never heard anything more beautiful in his life than her laugh. He'd never thought he'd hear it again.

Many hours later, after the doctor had given her scalp two stitches, bandaged her other cuts and pro-nounced her well, they made love several times more before they lay sleeping in each other's arms. Or rather, Kareef held her as she slept.

He couldn't stop looking at her.

Now, outside the window of his bedroom, he could see dawn rising over the desert, and his stomach growled. Time for breakfast, his body insisted. He realized he hadn't eaten at all yesterday. He smiled down at Jasmine sleeping in his arms and softly caressed her cheek. He'd been distracted.

He could hardly believe he already wanted her again. They'd barely slept at all last night. They'd made love at least four times, possibly four and a half, depending on what counted and what did not.

He should just hold her and sleep. He closed his eyes. Jasmine was the only woman he'd ever wanted close like this. He suddenly realized she was the only woman he'd ever slept with, in any sense of the word.

His arms tightened around her. Then his stomach growled again, louder this time. He glanced at her, surprised the sound hadn't startled her.

Kareef gave a resigned sigh. Careful not to wake her, he moved his arm from beneath her head and quietly dressed before he left her.

When she woke, he would surprise her. First with breakfast. He allowed himself a wicked smile. Then with dessert.

He went down the hallway to his modern kitchen and turned on the gas stove. Pulling pans off their hooks, he prepared eggs scrambled with meat, then toast and fruit. He got two plates from a cupboard and arranged them on a tray. As an afterthought, he went outside and picked a flower from the small pot of roses beside the front door.

When he came back into the house, he found Jasmine standing in the middle of the gleaming kitchen, wearing only an oversized T-shirt emblazoned with the name of some 1980s rock band.

"I couldn't find you," she said accusingly.

Leaning forward, he placed the rose in her hair,

tucking it behind her ear as he leaned forward to kiss her cheek. "I was hungry."

She smiled, looking somehow like a fairy princess in the large T-shirt with the flower in her mussed hair. "You're hungry an awful lot," she murmured.

Giving her a sensual grin, Kareef lifted a dark eyebrow. "You bring it out in me."

Her forehead furrowed as she searched his gaze. Then with an intake of breath she looked down at the tray. Her voice was soft, almost impossible to hear. "It looks delicious. Who made it?"

"I did."

She laughed, looking around the kitchen as if she expected to find three sous chefs hidden behind the huge refrigerator. "No. Really. Who made it?"

"I have no live-in staff here, Jasmine," he said. "I told you. I don't like being fussed over."

She looked at him skeptically, wrinkling her nose. "You mean to tell me—" she indicated the spotless, sparkling tile floor "—you mopped that yourself?"

"I'm independent—not insane," he said with a laugh. "I do have a housekeeper, as well as gardeners and my veterinary staff and stable workers. But they have their own cottages on the edge of my land. I live in this house alone. I prefer it that way."

"Oh."

"Let's go outside." Taking two cups of steaming Turkish coffee, he placed them on the tray beside the breakfast plates. Holding the patio door open with his shoulder, he carried the tray in one hand. "We can watch the sun rise."

She followed him out to the wooden deck behind the

kitchen. Leaning against the railing, she looked out at the vast expanse of desert stretching beyond the valley.

"You said you someday wanted to build a house out here," she whispered. "But I never imagined anything so beautiful as this."

Setting the tray down on the table, he looked at the dark, curvy silhouette of her body in front of the vast wide desert now glowing pink in the sunrise.

"Beautiful indeed," he said quietly.

She turned to face him. "It must be hard for you to leave this all behind."

A dull throb went through his head, in the back of his skull. "Yes."

He'd briefly forgotten the royal palace, forgotten the endless, unsatisfied crowds of people hemming him in, making demands of their king. Forgotten the fact that in just a few days, he would formally and forever renounce all right to be a private citizen with his own selfish desires. He would be king, sacrificing himself forever for the good of his people.

He took a deep breath. But today at least, he was home. He was free. He looked up at Jasmine, so impossibly beautiful in the old T-shirt that stretched over her breasts and barely covered her thighs. *Today at least he was with her.*

"Here, we can forget you are the king," she said softly. She turned back to lean against the railing, watching the pink sun peeking slowly over the violet mountains. "And I can forget I will be soon married."

Staring out blindly across the desert, she shivered in the cool morning.

Taking two cups of steaming coffee, he walked

across the deck to stand behind her. Handing her a mug, he wrapped one arm around her and pulled her back against his chest. He held her close as they watched the sun rise across the desert, filling the land with warmth and color like rose gold, as they both sipped coffee in silence.

She glanced back at him with a sudden embarrassed laugh. "You said you come here to be alone. Do you want me to go?"

He held her against his chest.

"No," he said quietly. "I want you to stay."

She didn't interrupt his solitude, he realized. She improved it. The quiet intimacy she offered him enriched everything, even the sunrise.

Looking out at the vast desert, he realized he was holding the only person on earth he'd ever wanted to be close to him. Not just in his bed, but in his life.

It couldn't last. He knew that. In just a few days, they would return to the city. Kareef would again become the king; Jasmine would become another man's wife. The magic would end.

But staring out at the streaks of orange sunlight now streaking across the brightening blue sky, Kareef told himself they had time. They had days left, hours and hours stretching ahead of them.

And surely, in this magical place, those days could last forever.

Two days later, Jasmine was floating on her back in the swimming pool, staring up at the bluest, widest sky on earth, when she felt Kareef rise up in the water beneath her, pulling her into his arms.

"Good morning," he growled. Rivulets of water trickled down the hard, tanned muscles of his chest as held her against him. "Why did you get up so early?" he whispered, nuzzling her neck. "You should have stayed in bed."

Looking down, she realized he was naked. And that there was something specific that he wanted from her.

"Early?" she teased, clinging to his shoulders and pretending to kick her feet in protest. "It's noon!"

"You kept me up 'til dawn, so it's your fault," he said, then all talk ceased as he kissed her. A few minutes later, still entwined in a kiss, he walked out of the pool with Jasmine's legs wrapped around his waist. Carrying her across the back patio, he laid her on the cushioned lounge bed beneath a loggia. There, he pulled off her string bikini and slowly made love to her in the open air, beneath the hot desert sun.

Afterward, Jasmine must have slept briefly in his arms, for when she opened her eyes, the sun had moved in the sky. But she no longer could recognize the line between sleeping and waking. How could she tell when she was sleeping, when everything she'd imagined in her heart's deepest dreams had become real, flesh and blood in her arms?

Her days here at Kareef's desert home had been drenched with laughter and tenderness and passion; her short stay here had been so full of color and life, they'd made the thirteen long years before seem nothing more than a lonely gray dream.

If only she could stay here forever.

Staring out at the reflected sunlight of the turquoise pool, she tried to push the thought from her mind. She had only one day left here. She should enjoy it. To-morrow morning, Kareef had to be back in the city. His diplomatic engagements could no longer be kept waiting; nor could he put off the royal banquet, which would be attended by the foreign dignitaries who'd come for his coronation.

Tonight, the dream would end.

Stop thinking about it, she tried to tell herself. *You'll only ruin the precious hours you have left.* But she couldn't stop herself. Even when she'd been in bed that morning, cuddled in Kareef's arms as he slept beside her, she'd stared up at the ceiling of his bed-room and wished with all her heart that she could stay here forever.

In his bed. In his arms.

She'd wished she could remain his wife.

The wish had been so powerful it had nearly choked her. And so she'd fled the bedroom and thrown herself into the pool, to stare up at the sky, to let the water and chlorine and hot sun dissolve her tears.

But now, as she held him on the lounge bed beneath the loggia beside the pool, she was almost tempted to ask him if there were any chance. Any chance at all. The words were trembling on her lips. Even though she already knew the answer.

"Kareef?" she whispered, then stopped.

"Hmm?" His face was pressed against hers, his body still naked beneath the sun. He didn't open his eyes. The sun had already half-dried the dark wave of his hair.

She took a deep breath. "I was…I was wondering…"

Then a sparkle caught her eye. She looked out by the pool and saw the pants he'd discarded carelessly before he'd jumped into the water. Something had tumbled out of the pocket, now glistening green in the light.

The emerald.

The tiny heart-shaped emerald on a gold chain her parents had given her for her sixteenth birthday. She'd been wearing it when Kareef had asked her to marry him that day in the thicket of trees behind the riding school. According to the ancient Qusani ritual, she'd been required to give a token as pledge of her faith. So she'd pulled the gold chain off her neck, and placed it in his hand as she'd tearfully spoken the words that would bind them.

And now, after thirteen years, he was carelessly carrying the necklace around in his pants pocket, awaiting the moment he would divorce her.

Staring at the emerald glinting in the sun, she blinked hard as all her dreams came crashing around her.

Kareef lifted his head. "What is it?" he said lazily, his hand lingering on her breast. He sighed. "Don't tell me. Do you already want more?" He yawned, but was already smiling as he reached for her. "You tire me out, woman...."

She closed her eyes. She *did* want more. More of him. More of everything. And she suddenly couldn't allow him to touch her—not when she felt like crying, thrashing, wailing like a child for what she could never have.

He stopped. "Jasmine?"

"It's nothing," she whispered. "I'm just—" her voice broke *"—happy."*

"As am I." Kareef's hand suddenly tightened on her own. "But you know our time cannot last."

Her eyes flew open. Already? She wasn't ready for

him to speak the words. Her eyes fell upon the emerald necklace hanging out of his pocket in the shorts crumpled by the pool. She wasn't ready! Not yet!

With a nimbleness born of fear, she leapt to her feet, backing away. "It's a beautiful day. Shall we go for a ride?"

The way his jaw dropped would have been comical, if her heart weren't breaking.

"A ride?" he repeated in shock.

"Horse riding," she explained succinctly.

Frowning in bewilderment, he rubbed the back of his head. "But you hate riding. You…hate it."

Was he remembering the same thing she was, of their long-ago horse ride in the desert? Of how he'd found her, thrown on the rocks after his horse Razul had been spooked by a snake? Kareef had fallen to his knees before her, his eyes dark with fear, his face pale and streaked with dirt beneath the red twilight. *"Hold on, Jasmine,"* he'd whispered as he'd carried her to the cave. *"Just hold on.…"*

Lifting her chin, she swallowed, pushing the memory away. "I don't hate riding," she said flatly.

"Since when?"

Her eyes flashed at him. "I've been gone a long time."

"Have you changed so much?"

"How about we race, and see?"

"You—race against me?" He laughed. "You're kidding, right?"

"Are you scared?" she taunted in reply.

His face grew serious. He rose to his feet. Standing naked in front of her, beneath the shadows of the loggia, he cupped her face in his hands.

"You don't have to do this, Jasmine." His tender blue gaze, endless as the desert sky, whispered through her soul. "You don't have anything to prove."

"I know." In his arms, beneath the deep intensity of his glance, she could feel her heart break with yearning to be his wife. Not just today, but forever. With a sharp intake of breath, she forced herself to pull away. "Race you to the stables!"

She hurried to their bedroom and ransacked the bottom of her suitcase. *I'll just enjoy this last day,* she vowed to herself. *I'll emblazon it forever on my heart.* Throwing on underwear beneath a long white cotton dress of eyelet lace, she quickly ran a brush through her long dark hair and ran out of the house.

A few minutes later, when Kareef appeared at the stables dressed in black pants and a white shirt, she'd already climbed into the saddle. When Kareef saw the horse she'd chosen, he stopped in his tracks.

"Not that one."

"She's the one I want," Jasmine replied steadily.

Kareef glowered down at the wizened old horse master with skin like tanned leather who'd assisted her into the saddle.

"Bara'ah is the one she chose, sire," the Qusani said with a shrug, his raspy voice tinged with the ancient dialect of Qais. "Give your lady the freedom of your house, you said. Obey her every whim, you said."

Caught by his own command, Kareef scowled at them both.

Jasmine beamed back at him. She was determined to show them both how much she'd changed over the last thirteen years. She was strong. Independent. She didn't need him to protect her as she once had, and she would prove that. *To both of them.*

Kareef stepped toward her, looking up. "Not this mare, Jasmine. Bara'ah is full of tricks. You saw how she escaped her paddock—she caused the car accident."

"She didn't do it on purpose." She patted the horse's neck sympathetically. "She was just tired of being trapped behind walls."

"Jasmine—"

"You're already losing the race," she said, and lightly kicked the black mare's sides. The horse sprung forward, flying out of the stable, leaving Kareef cursing behind her.

He caught up with her five minutes later across the flatlands, when she slowed the mare down to a controlled trot.

"You *do* know how to ride," he said grudgingly. "Where did you learn?"

She gave him a sweet smile. "New York."

She'd taken lessons in Westchester County, spending her free time riding in Central Park. She'd learned to ride English style, Western style, even Qusani bareback. She'd hoped it would stop her nightmares, stop her from dreams where she hit the ground and woke up with the taste of blood in her mouth.

It hadn't. But at least she had learned a new skill. It gave her great pleasure now to ride beside Kareef as his equal, with confidence and skill. Especially in this beautiful place.

Qais was so stark and savage, she thought, looking around her. Some might have found the vast open landscape bleak, but she felt freedom. She no longer felt hemmed in by skyscrapers that blocked her vision, that blocked the sun.

Here, in every direction, Jasmine could see a horizon. *She felt free.*

"Come on," she said playfully, turning her reins in a new direction. She had no idea where she was going, but she loved not knowing. "On the mark…get set…*go*!"

She took off at a gallop into the desert, and Kareef pursued her.

Jasmine was ahead of him for about three seconds before his stallion whooshed past her. She followed, clinging to Bara'ah's back with every ounce of her determination. But Kareef had been a horse racer since childhood, and he was on a bigger, faster horse; her ten years of practice could not compete with his glorious fearless speed.

Whirling around, he pulled in front of her with a grin. "I win."

"Yes," she sighed. "You win."

"And so I take my prize." Drawing his horse beside hers, he leaned over and kissed her in the saddle. It was a hard, demanding kiss that left her aching for more.

When he pulled away, she stared at him in shock.

Here in the desert, the sun burned away all lies. As she stared at his beautiful, strong, arrogant face, everything suddenly became clear.

She loved him.

She always had, and she always would.

Jasmine gripped the pommel of her saddle, blinking, staggered by the realization.

Smiling, Kareef reached out to stroke her cheek.

"You kiss like you ride. Like a wanton," he murmured appreciatively. He looked down at her intently. "Jasmine," he said in a low voice, "you have to know that I…"

Then his eyes suddenly focused on something in the distance behind her. His hand dropped from her cheek. He sat back stiffly in his saddle.

"What is it?" she whispered, staring at him.

Clenching his jaw, he nodded to a spot behind her. "The house where you will live. Hajjar's house."

She twisted in the saddle and gasped. Far on the horizon, she saw an enormous monstrosity of a mansion, a red stone castle with red flags flying from the turrets. She blinked at it in horror.

"He's not there," he said quietly behind her. "They're not at home."

"So where are they?" she whispered. "Where did they go?"

Kareef exhaled, hissing through his teeth. She heard him shift in the saddle. "Don't like the look of those clouds," he said. "See them?"

Desert sandstorms were the subject of scary tales told to Qusani children, so Jasmine looked sharply at the horizon. The sky had indeed darkened to a deep gray-brown; but she could barely look past Umar's hideous red castle to see the clouds. Comparing the hideous red edifice to Kareef's simple home in the oasis, she wanted to weep. But she wouldn't let Kareef see her cry. Couldn't!

"Jasmine, we should go back," Kareef said quietly behind her. "Then we need to talk."

She whirled back in the saddle. She saw his hand already reaching in his pocket. She sucked in her breath. In another moment, he'd pull out the emerald necklace. He only needed to hand it to her and speak three words to separate them forever.

Irony. The same hour she'd realized she loved him, he would divorce her.

She would marry Umar and be his trophy wife, caged in this monstrous red castle and other sprawling mansions just like it in luxurious locations around the world.

She would have respectability. She would have a family.

But at the price of her soul.

Kareef's eyes narrowed as he again stared past her toward the horizon. "We must hurry. Come now."

With a low whistle, he whirled his horse around and tore into a gallop, clearly expecting her to follow.

She watched him for one instant.

"No," she whispered. "I won't."

She turned her reins in the opposite direction. With a sharp voice in the mare's ear, she leaned forward, pushing her heels hard against the mare's sides. With a snort, the horse flew.

"Jasmine!" Kareef shouted behind her. "What are you doing? Come back!"

But she wouldn't. She couldn't even look back. Love was burning her like acid, bubbling away her soul.

Tightening her knees, she held her body low and tight against the horse's back, riding up the red canyon. Riding for her life.

CHAPTER SEVEN

KAREEF gasped as he saw Jasmine leap her horse across a juniper bush, sweeping across the sagebrush. She'd once been terrified of horses. Now she rode with the grace and natural ease of a Qusani nomad.

He stared in shock at the cloud of her dust crossing the desert.

But she didn't know that devious mare like he did. There was a reason Bara'ah wasn't north at the stadium, training to race in the Qais Cup in two days' time. She'd left one jockey in a body cast last year. Full of malicious tricks, she liked nothing more than to throw her riders.

He had the sudden image of Jasmine half-smashed on the rock, crumpled and bleeding, as he'd found her thirteen years ago….

"Jasmine! Stop!"

He saw her goad her mare into greater speed.

Fear rushed through him as he glanced back again at the distant horizon and saw scattered brown clouds moving fast, much too fast. A sandstorm could cross the desert in seconds, decimating everything in its path.

A shudder went through his body. He turned back. With iron control, he clicked his heels on the stallion's flanks. Huffing with a flare of nostril, the animal raced forward. But Jasmine was already far ahead.

Kareef hadn't expected her to disobey him. No one had disobeyed him for years.

He should have expected it of her.

As he pursued her, he cast another glance behind him. The clouds were beginning to gather with force across the width of the desert. The sky was turning dark. There could no longer be any doubt. Holding the reins with one hand, he reached into his pocket and discovered his cell phone was lost, fallen in the rough speed of their race. But he still had Jasmine's necklace.

His eyes narrowed as he watched her race her horse headlong into the canyon. No help could come for them before the storm.

So be it. He would save her alone.

As long as she stayed hidden, as long as she didn't climb up out of the canyon, she would live.

If she rode onto the plateau, the coming sandstorm would eat her alive.

Hoofbeats pounded in rhythm with Kareef's thoughts as he raced after Jasmine into the dark shadowed canyon.

He had to find her.

He *would* find her.

Clamping his thigh muscles over the saddle, he leaned forward and urged his horse faster. He'd spent his youth in these canyons. He was again a reckless horse racer who feared nothing…but losing her.

He raced fast. Faster. His stallion kicked up dust,

scattering it to the four winds. He raced beneath the sharp arches and towering cliffs of the canyon.

Within minutes, he'd caught up with her. Leaning forward, he shouted Jasmine's name over the pounding hoofbeats of their horses.

She glanced back and a shadow of fear crossed her face. He heard the panic in her voice as she urged her mare faster.

But Kareef gained ground with every second. He reached out his hand to pluck her off the mare's back—

His hand suddenly grasped air as she veered off the road. She'd abruptly turned the mare west through a break in the red rock, climbing the slope up out of the canyon.

"No!" he shouted. "The storm!"

But his words were lost in the rising blur of the wind, beneath the pounding hooves of her mare's wild, joyful, reckless climb.

He could feel, rather than hear, the approaching storm behind him. The first edges of dark cloud pushed around them, turning blue sky to a sickening brown-gray. The crags were turning dark and hidden in deep shadows.

Cursing her, cursing himself, he veered his horse up to pursue her. She was fast, but he was faster. For the first time in thirteen years, he was again Kareef Al'Ramiz, the reckless horse racer. Unstoppable. Unbreakable.

He would die rather than lose this race.

"Sandstorm!" he shouted over the rising wind.

At the top of the plateau, Jasmine turned back to him sharply. But at the same moment, he saw her mare draw to a sudden skidding stop as she suddenly grew tired of the race and deliberately, almost playfully, threw her rider. For a long, horrible instant, Kareef watched Jasmine fly through the air.

Sniffing, the mare jumped delicately in the other direction, then turned to run back the way she'd come, toward the stables and oats that awaited her.

Jasmine hit the ground and crumpled into the dust. Kareef's heart was in his throat as all the memories of the past ripped through him. He flung himself off his stallion, falling to his knees before her.

"Jasmine," he whispered, his heart in his throat as he touched her still face. "Jasmine!"

Like a miracle, she coughed in his arms. Her beautiful, dark-lashed eyes stared up at him. She swallowed, tried to speak.

"Don't talk," he ordered. Relief made his body weak as he lifted her in his arms. He held her tightly, never wanting to let her go. How had he spent so many years without her? How could he have known she was alive…without tracking her to the last corner of the earth?

He heard the distant rattle of sand and thunder, heard the wail of the wind.

"I have to get you out of here." He whistled to the horse. "We don't have much time."

He glanced behind them. The safe part of the canyon was too far away. They'd never make it.

Jasmine followed his glance and instantly went pale when she saw the dark wall of cloud. "I thought—" her voice choked off "—I thought it was a trick."

She'd grown up in Qusay. She knew what a sandstorm could do. He shook his head grimly, clenching his jaw. "We have to find shelter." His eyes met hers. "The closest shelter."

Her chocolate-brown eyes instantly went wide with panic. "No," she gasped. "Not there, Kareef. I'd rather die!"

He felt the first scattered bits of sand hit his face.

"If I don't get you to safety right now," he said grimly, "you *will* die."

Whimpering, she shook her head. But he knew she had to see the darkness swiftly overtaking the sun, had to feel the shards of sand whipping against her skin. If they didn't find shelter, they'd soon be breathing sand. It would rip off their skin, then bury them alive.

"No!" she screamed, kicking and struggling as, holding her with one arm, he lifted them both into the saddle. "I can't go back!"

"I can't leave you to die," he ground out, turning the horse's reins toward the nearby cliff.

"I died a long time ago." Her eyes were wet, her voice hoarse as she stared at the dark jagged hole, hollowed and hidden in the red rock. "I died in that cave."

The pain he heard in her voice was insidious, like a twisting cloud of smoke. He breathed in her grief, felt it infect his own body.

Jasmine Kouri. Once his life. Once his *everything*.

Then his eyes hardened. "I can't let you die."

She twisted around in the saddle, wrapping her arms around his neck as she looked up at his face pleadingly. "Please," she whispered, her eyes shimmering with tears. "If you ever loved me—if you ever loved me at all—don't take me there."

He looked down at her beautiful face, and his heart stopped in his chest.

If he'd ever loved her?

He'd loved her more than a man should ever love any woman. More than a man should love anything he couldn't bear to lose. Looking down at her now, he would have given her anything, his own life, to make her stop weeping.

Then he saw a drop of blood appear on the pale skin of her cheek, like a red rose springing from the earth. First blood.

A growl ripped from his throat. His own life he would give. But not hers. *Not hers.*

Ignoring her cries, he grimly urged the black stallion toward the plateau to the red rock cliff. The sounds of her wailing blended with the howls of the wind. He felt prickles of sand start to abrade his skin with tiny cuts.

He held her against his chest, protecting her with his own body as he rode straight for the one place he never wanted to see again. The place where they'd both lost everything thirteen years ago. His own private hell.

Hardening his heart to granite, he rode straight for the cave.

"No!" Jasmine screamed in his arms, struggling to jump off the horse's back. But Kareef wouldn't let her go.

She felt the bone-jarring pounding of the stallion's gallop beneath her. She felt the heat of Kareef's chest at her back, felt his strong arms protecting her as the flecks of sand began to snarl around them with deadly force.

The howl of the wind grew louder. Her dark hair

flew wildly around her face. She closed her eyes, fighting the rising tide of fear. He was taking her to the cave. The place that had terrified her beyond reason for a thousand nightmares.

"We'll make it," Kareef said harshly, as if he could make it true by the sheer force of his will. His shout was a whisper above the wail of the storm.

Looking back, she saw a wall of sand pouring like a massive dark cloud behind them, a black blizzard sweeping across the wide plateau, leaving nothing in its wake.

They reached the cave just in time. He pulled her off the horse, yanking them back some distance inside the darkness. Stumbling, she watched the huge wave of wind and sand pass the mouth of the cave, leaving them coughing in a cloud of dust.

Staggering back, she looked blindly behind her into the black maw of the cave. And against her will…

She saw the spot where she'd lost their baby.

Pain racked through her, pummeling her like a torrent of blows. Anguish broke over her, as devastating as the wall of sand outside, crushing her soul beneath the weight.

As Kareef turned to calm the stallion, tying his reins to a nearby rock, Jasmine's trembling legs gave way beneath her. She fell back against the red stone walls, sliding down to the ground, unable to look away from the spot of earth where she'd nearly died.

Where she *had* died.

Across the cave, she saw Kareef gently calm the stallion, whispering words in ancient Qusani as he removed the pack from the horse's haunches. He offered the horse water and food then brushed down the horse in long strokes. The sound of the brushing filled the silence of the cave. She stared at him.

Kareef always took care of everything he loved. What a father he would make.

But they could never share a child.

Not a day went by that Jasmine didn't think about the baby she'd lost in the riding accident before she'd even known she was pregnant. Their child would have been twelve now. A little boy with his father's blue eyes? A little girl with plump cheeks and a sweet smile?

As Kareef started a fire in the fire pit with wood left recently by Qusani nomads, a sob rose from deep inside her.

"I'm sorry," she whispered, looking up as tears spilled down her cheeks. "It's my fault I lost our baby."

She heard his harsh intake of breath, and suddenly his arms were around her. Sitting against the wall of the cave, he lifted her into his lap, holding her against his chest as tenderly as a child.

"It was never your fault. Never," he said in a low voice. "I am the only one who was to blame—"

His voice choked off as the small fire flickered light into the depths of the cave, casting red shadows over the earth. She looked up at him slowly. His face was blurry in the firelight.

She blinked, and the pain in his eyes overwhelmed her. She could hear the roar of the wind and hoarse rattle of the sand against rock outside. Instinctively, she reached out to stroke the dark hair of his bowed head. Then she stopped herself.

"You broke your promise to me, Kareef," she said hoarsely. "You brought a doctor to this cave, after you gave your word to tell no one. Though we both knew it was too late!"

"You were dying, Jasmine!" He looked up fiercely. "I was a fool to make that promise, a fool to think I could take care of you alone, a fool to think that love alone could save you!"

"But when I lost your child and the ability to ever conceive," she said numbly, "you couldn't get away from me fast enough."

His hands suddenly clenched around her shoulders. The dark rage in his eyes frightened her.

"I left to die," he ground out. With a hoarse, ragged intake of breath, he released her, clawing his hand through his black hair. "I failed you. I couldn't bear to see the blame and grief in your eyes. *I went out to the desert to die.*"

His voice echoed in the cool darkness of the cave.

He'd tried to die—the strong, powerful, fearless boy she'd loved? The barbarian king she'd once thought to be indestructible?

"No," she said, "you wouldn't."

"One more thing I failed to do."

Bewildered, she looked up at his handsome face, half-hidden by the shadows. "But…it wasn't your fault."

"I was the one who saddled Razul for you! I was the one who taunted you into climbing on his back! I wanted so badly to race with you." He gave a bitter laugh. "I thought I could keep you safe."

"Kareef." Her voice was a sob. "Stop."

But he was beyond hearing. "After the accident, I

let you stay here in the cave for days, injured, without a doctor's care. You nearly died from the infection."

"I was trying to protect my family from the shame—"

"I brought the doctor too late, and never thought to worry about his assistant." He gave a bitter laugh—brittle, like dead leaves blowing in the wind. "Afterward, when I disappeared into the desert, I left you believing you'd be happier without me, safe and protected by your family. It never occurred to me that the scandal could break and you'd be sent into exile. You'd already been in New York for three years before I even heard you'd left Qusay!" He leaned forward, his jaw tight. His eyes were dark in the flickering fire. "But I made him pay for what he did to you."

Her full, pink lips trembled. "Who?"

"Marwan. When I discovered he was the one who'd started the rumors, I stripped him of everything he owned. I sent him into exile."

A small sound escaped her lips. A rush, like a shuddering sigh. "Thank you," she whispered. "Did you know he blackmailed me?"

"What?"

"On my journey back to the city, when I still had a fever, he threatened to tell everyone about my miscarriage. He said he'd claim I did it deliberately to rid myself of the baby. He'd say I'd had endless nameless lovers and couldn't guess the father. He said he would ruin me." She took a deep breath, forcing her eyes to meet his. "He would do this—unless I took him as my lover."

Kareef sucked in his breath.

"What?" he exploded.

"He was afraid of you," she said softly, wiping her eyes hard. "But he wasn't afraid of me. When I wouldn't do it, he carried through with his threat. Within days, the scandal cost my father his job at the palace. It gave his enemies the weapon they needed. If my father couldn't control his own family, they said, how could he advise the king? So everything that happened, it's my fault, you see." She took a deep, shuddering breath. "All my fault."

She looked back at Kareef.

And almost didn't recognize him.

Rage such as she'd never seen before was on his face. Rage that frightened her.

"I will kill him," he ground out. Clenching his hands, he rose to his feet. "Wherever that man is hiding in the world, I will make him feel such pain as he cannot imagine—"

"No," she gasped, grabbing his hand. "Please. It's all over." She pressed his hand against her forehead, closing her eyes. "Please, I just want to forget."

His hand tightened, then relaxed. Slowly, he sank beside her. Kneeling, he took both her hands in his own.

"By the time I found out you were in exile…it was too late to do more than send money to New York." His voice was ragged. "But every day since then, I've tried to find absolution." He turned away. "But I know now I will never find that, no matter how hard I try."

"Kareef," she whispered, tears in her eyes. "It wasn't your fault. It was… It was…" Putting her hand on his shoulder, she stared at the smooth rock wall of the cave and the truth dawned on her. "It was an accident."

His back slowly straightened. "What did you say?"

"An accident." She looked at him, and it was as if the sun had broken through dark clouds, bringing light, bringing peace. Tears fell down her cheeks as she breathed, "I was barely pregnant. We didn't know. The accident was no one's fault. No one is to blame. We'll never forget we almost had a child. But we need to forgive—both of us. It wasn't your fault."

His voice was low and thick with grief as he said, "I wish I could believe that." He looked down at her hands. "You're shivering."

She was, but not with cold.

Rising to his feet, he crossed the cave. Digging through the horse's pack, he found a red woven blanket and unfolded it near the fire. Jasmine watched his face in the flickering shadows, her heart aching.

All these years, she thought he'd blamed her—and he'd thought the same.

For her, it had been thirteen years of exile.

For him, it had been a living death.

"Here," he said in a low voice. "You can rest here, where it is warm." He turned away. "I will stay awake and keep watch until the storm is over."

Trembling, Jasmine rose to her feet. She slowly walked toward him. Reaching up, she placed a hand on his cheek and forced him to look at her.

"It was an accident, Kareef," she said, looking straight into his eyes. "You were not to blame!"

He gave a hoarse intake of breath. "Is it possible you could forgive me?" he whispered, searching her gaze. His blue eyes were deep and endless as the sea.

She stroked his cheek with her hand. Tears filled her eyes. "How could I blame you? You were…have always been—" *my only love*, her voice choked "—my dearest friend."

She heard his ragged breath, felt the pounding of his heart against hers. His body was hot. His skin smelled of musk and sun and sand.

He looked down at her, and his gaze suddenly burned through her, stretching every nerve from her fingertips to her toes in taut anticipation as she heard the howl of the darkness outside. "And you are mine."

Lowering his head, he kissed her.

Hidden in this cave, hidden far from the outside world and protected from the outside storm, he kissed her as if nothing and no one else existed. He pressed her against the smooth red rock wall of the cave, and she kissed him back fervently, her heart on her lips.

He abruptly pulled away from her. She blinked at him in the flickering firelight, dazed. His eyes were dark with need. Her lips felt swollen and bruised from the ferocity of his kisses—almost as bruised as her healing heart.

With a growl, he lifted her up into his arms, holding her against his hard chest as if she weighed nothing at all. She stared up at him, breathless, mesmerized by his brutal strength. She could hear the howl of the wind whipping sand outside, hear the whinny of the stallion. The small fire flickered shadowy firelight against the smooth red rock of the cave.

They were safe here. They were warm. They were together.

He lowered her gently to the blanket, then pulled off his white shirt and black pants and shoes. She gazed at his naked body in wonder as he stood before her. The muscles of his tanned body glistened in the twisting firelight.

Kneeling in front of her on the blanket, he slowly pulled off her panties beneath her dress, drawing them down her legs.

Then, with a wicked half smile, he tossed them into the fire.

"What?" she spluttered, staring at the white cotton fabric now burning beside the charred wood. "What did you do that for?"

He lifted a black eyebrow, giving her a dark look that curled her toes. "We needed fuel for the fire," he whispered.

But a fire was already burning inside Jasmine, burning right through her, consuming her whole. He pulled her down into his lap, pulling her white skirt up to her hips. She was naked against him as he slid his hardness against her, rocking back and forth against her wet core. He leaned up to kiss her.

Hot. *Hot.* She was burning up, turning to ash and flame.

"Take off my dress," she whispered. "Take it off."

"You," he repeated approvingly, sliding his hands over her breasts as he nipped little kisses up her neck, "are a wanton."

With a tug, he pulled the white cotton dress up and over her shoulders and threw it down on the earth. She sat in his lap, her legs wrapped around his waist. She looked down at their naked intertwined bodies in the firelight. As he started to move against her, the soft sound of her gasps soon matched the cries of the wind outside.

The tension coiled low in her belly as he slid over

her. Pleasure built inside her and then, suddenly, he lifted her up and impaled her with a single deep thrust. She gasped at the depth of his penetration.

He hadn't just filled her body. He filled her soul.

She gripped his shoulders and let the ecstasy build inside her, higher and higher. Even when the euphoria finally ripped her to shreds, exploding her into pieces, she kept her secret hidden inside.

I love you.

I will always love you.

She couldn't speak the words. She knew they changed nothing.

CHAPTER EIGHT

For an instant Kareef was afraid he'd hurt her. Then she moaned, swaying against him, tightening her legs around his waist as he filled her.

He gasped at that movement, at the way her full breasts brushed against his chest. Then he pushed her down again, thrusting inside her, filling her so deeply a growl escaped the back of his throat.

Firelight cast shadows over her beautiful face, her full, swollen lips, and the long dark eyelashes tightly closed in an expression of joy. Watching her, he held his breath with the effort it took to hold himself back.

He was inside her, but she was the one who filled him.

Jasmine. Her beauty. Her boundless sensuality. She swayed against him with the decadent grace of a houri. Beads of sweat were like clear pearls on her white, swanlike neck as she leaned back, gasping. The veil of her dark, glossy hair cascaded down her back, swinging back and forth as she kept her eyes closed, panting for breath.

Lifting her head with his hand, he kissed her. She gasped her pleasure against his mouth, gripping his shoulders, biting into his flesh with her fingernails, marking him in her own act of possession.

The force of his taking was primal—unstoppable. He heard her cry out and could hold back no longer. He gripped her against his body as he poured himself into her with a shout.

He collapsed back on the red blanket, holding her against him. He did not know when he woke. She was still sleeping in his arms.

They were both naked. The fire was dying. The night was growing cold, the darkness growing around them.

He felt her shiver. He looked down at her face. She was sleeping, her cheek pressed against his chest. Her beauty went beyond her dark hair or perfect pink lips. It went deeper than her pale skin with roses in her cheeks.

Even after all the times he'd made love to her, he did not feel satiated. And he was starting to fear he never would be.

He did not want to divorce her.

Silently, Kareef withdrew himself from beneath her body and rose to his feet. Crossing the cave, he pulled a second blanket from the horse's pack. Crawling back beside her, he covered them both with it, wrapping her in his arms. He knew, even in sleep, he would not let her go.

Growing drowsy, he looked down at her sleeping against him. He wanted her like this every night. In his bed. At his table. On his arm. Charming diplomats with her beauty. Dancing in his arms.

With her beauty and gentle grace, Jasmine would be the perfect queen. But…

His jaw tightened as he stared at the dying fire.

He still had to divorce her. He had to provide an heir of the blood. The Al'Ramizes had reigned Qusay for a thousand years. His cousin Xavian had given up the throne when he'd learned he was a changeling, a substitute for a lost Al'Ramiz child.

Blood meant everything. It gave the Al'Ramiz men the right to rule. Not just the right—the obligation. And Jasmine could never become pregnant with his child.

His throat became tight. He looked away, staring at the bumps and rocks of scattered earth illuminated by the fading embers of the fire. Outside, he could hear the rattle of the sand against the solid rocks of the cliffs, hear the wind wailing in disappointed fury as it slowly died.

He slept fitfully, holding her tight.

"Kareef." Her naked body stirred in his arms. "Are you awake?"

Her voice was like a dream, full of sweet warmth, offering such peace. He slowly opened his eyes.

At the mouth of the cave, above the piles of new sand, he saw the gray light of dawn creeping over the western mountains. The wind had died down. The desert was calm. He could hear the plaintive sound of morning birds, hear the soft whinny of the stallion hungry for breakfast.

It was morning. The storm was over.

Their time was over.

Unwillingly, he turned to Jasmine. Her face was like cool water, a balm to his spirit. Her brown eyes reflected deep pools of light. But it only made the pain worse.

He did not want to let her go.

"It's barely dawn," he lied softly. His arms tightened around her. "Go back to sleep."

For a moment, she rested against him, and silence fell in the cool darkness of the cave. Then she shifted in his arms and her head popped up to look down at him. "Do you think your men are looking for us?"

"Yes," he said. "They will be here soon."

He heard her intake of breath, felt her pull away from him on the blanket. When she spoke, her voice was curiously flat. "Then it's time."

"Time?"

"Time for you to divorce me."

He looked up at her. Her expression had turned to stone, the pools of light shuttered and gone. She glanced over at the black fabric now crumpled on the other side of the cave.

"I know you have the emerald," she whispered.

"Yes," he said, his jaw tight. "I brought it with me."

"So eager to be rid of me?"

"I promised to set you free."

She lifted her chin, her expression a mixture of bravado and pain. "So do it."

Kareef's hands tightened into fists.

Jasmine was right. It was time. The storm was over, and his men were no doubt grimly combing the desert. Soon, they'd be found, and Kareef would return to Shafar. Back to the royal palace, back to his endless duties. He would be hosting a royal banquet tonight.

Then, tomorrow, he would attend the Qais Cup. And witness the wedding of Jasmine Kouri to Umar Hajjar.

It was dawn. The magic was over.

"Kareef?" Jasmine looked at him, her eyes swimming with misery.

She felt the same as he did, he realized. She did not want this divorce.

The knowledge flooded him with sudden strength. So he would not give her up. Not yet. *He wasn't done with her yet.*

"No," he growled. "I won't speak the words yet."

"But Kareef," she choked out, "you know you must!"

"Must?" He sat up. His shoulders straightened as his whole body became as unyielding as steel. He looked down at her, as selfish and ruthless and harsh as any ancient sultan.

"There is no *must*," he growled, lifting his chin as his eyes glittered down at her. "I'm the king of Qusay. And until I release you, *you belong to me.*"

You belong to me.

Jasmine shivered at the words. She could not deny them. She did belong to Kareef. She always had, body and soul.

But he was king of Qusay. He could not keep a barren woman as his bride. And she couldn't openly remain his mistress. Such a scandal would make the one thirteen years ago seem like nothing.

Jasmine closed her eyes with a shuddering breath. She'd returned to Qusay to help her family, not ruin them again! And how could she stab Umar in the heart with such a public humiliation, after everything he'd done for her?

They had to divorce. They had to part. There was no other way. If she allowed herself to be with Kareef as she wished—if she allowed herself to be *selfish*—it would destroy everyone she loved. She looked up at Kareef.

Already, a team of his bodyguards was searching, no doubt panicked that their king had disappeared in the sandstorm.

Was that a helicopter she heard in the distance now? *No*, she told herself frantically. *Not yet!*

But she had to face the hard truth. Their sweet, stolen time was over.

Pushing away from Kareef's warmth, she rose numbly to her feet. It was too late for her panties—they'd been annihilated in the fire—but she pulled on her white cotton bra, which she found on the floor of the cave.

"You don't need that," Kareef said, lying back against the blanket. "We have hours yet. It's barely dawn."

She didn't answer.

Kareef pushed himself up on one elbow. "Jasmine."

She didn't look back. She was afraid if she looked into the basilisk intensity of his gaze, she would be caught by his magic once again and lose her own ability to do what must be done. Even now, her body shook with the effort of defying him—and worse, defying her own deepest longings.

She found the white cotton dress, now dirty and with tiny rips in the eyelet lace, crumpled behind a rock. It seemed eons since he'd pulled it off her body.

So much had happened since then. Entire worlds had changed.

She felt his gaze, but wouldn't turn to meet his eyes.

Naked, he sprang lightly to his feet, like a warrior. Taking her in his arms, he forced her to turn around and meet his gaze. "What is it? What's wrong?"

She swallowed. "Thank you for these beautiful days in the desert," she whispered, feeling like her heart was splitting, bleeding in her chest. "I will never forget them."

"Our time is not over."

Trembling, Jasmine closed her eyes. It would be easier to say this if she didn't have to look at his beautifully masculine face, at his sensual mouth, at his eyes of endless blue. He took her heart apart in his gaze.

"It is over," she whispered. "We are over."

She felt his shock. Felt his hands go slack before he tightened his grip painfully around her. "Look at me."

She wouldn't.

"Look at me!"

Compelled to obey, she opened her eyes.

His face was dark with fury.

"You are mine, Jasmine. For as long as I want you."

Her throat went dry. How she wished it could be true, wished she could be his forever—or for even one more night!

"How?" she replied hoarsely. "How can I be yours, Kareef?"

His eyes darkened and cooled until they were like a thousand storms over the Arctic Sea. "You bound yourself to me long ago."

"Kareef—"

"You will not marry him tomorrow. It is too soon!"

Her tortured eyes flickered up at him. "What would you have me do, then? Desert Umar at the altar? Be your mistress? Leave my family to their ruin?"

His jaw clenched. "We could keep our affair a secret—"

"There's no such thing at the palace!" she cried.

"Here in the desert, perhaps, with only your trusted servants, we could keep it quiet for a short while. But you know as well as I do that there are no secrets at the royal palace. There's likely gossip about us already. I've already caused my family so much pain, and now my little sister is pregnant. How could my parents ever hold up their heads in the street, if I let myself be branded as your whore?"

Air hissed through his teeth.

"No one would call you that," he raged. "You would be respected as my…as my—"

"As your what? As your wife? We cannot remain married. You know we cannot!"

His eyes glittered down at her. "I can do as I please. I am the king."

She heard a distant helicopter, a deep *flick-flick-flick* high above the desert, and this time there could be no doubt. Shaking her head, she gave a harsh laugh.

"For a man with your sense of honor," she said, fighting back tears, "that makes you less free than the lowliest servant in your palace."

"Jasmine…"

"No!" she shouted. "I cannot back out of my engagement. Umar would be humiliated. My family's reputation would be destroyed. First my scandal, then Nima's pregnancy—my parents would never be able to leave their house again!"

"Why do you even care, after the way they've treated you?"

"Because I love them. Because—" she lifted her head as tears filled her eyes "—they are the only family I'll ever have. They, and Umar and his children. I cannot be the cause of their ruin by becoming your whore!"

"Don't use that word! I would kill any man who called you that!"

"All of them?" Her throat tightened as a hoarse laugh escaped her. "You would kill your own subjects for speaking the truth?"

His hands clenched her shoulders. "It's not the truth, and you know it!"

She briefly closed her eyes, trying to regain her strength, to catch her breath. "What else would you call an engaged woman who's done what I've done with you?"

"You've done nothing wrong. You're my wife."

"Let me go, Kareef," she whispered. "Set me free."

He looked down at her, his eyes full of an impetuous mixture of autocratic male possessiveness and emotion that struck her to the heart. "I can protect you, Jasmine."

"How?" she whispered, then shook her head. "Even you cannot work miracles—"

"It's a miracle you're here with me now." Cupping her face, he looked down at her. "And I will not let you go. Not yet."

She felt his rough fingertips against her skin. Felt his naked body, so warm and hard and fierce against hers. Felt how much he desired her. Felt the power of his savage strength as he lowered his mouth to hers.

His lips moved against hers with deep, exquisite tenderness. Persuading her. Mastering her, not just with his sensual power, but with the ache of her own body and heart.

When he finally released her, a low sigh rose from

her throat. She gazed up at him, this man she loved, feeling dazed and warm, drenched by the soft sunlight of his nearness.

His kiss had conquered her as a thousand words could not.

Exhaling, he pulled her back against his bare chest, stroking her hair as he felt her surrender. "You're mine, Jasmine," he murmured into her hair, almost too softly for her to hear. "As I am yours."

Distantly, a voice cried inside her that he wasn't hers—that he could never be hers, not anymore. And that by going back to Shafar with him as his secret mistress, she'd be risking everything she held precious—everyone she loved.

But she could not let him go. Not yet. Not yet!

She closed her eyes as he held her in her arms. *Let the future come as it will*, she thought. Somehow, they could find a way to be together just for a little while longer without hurting anyone. Couldn't they?

The helicopter was very loud now. She saw the swirl of sand outside the cave turn by the force of its rotor blades as it landed on the nearby plateau.

Jasmine pulled back with sudden alarm. "Get dressed. We can't let your men find you naked…alone with me!"

He snorted a laugh. "That would be a most unexpected sight for them, wouldn't it?"

Picking up his clothes from the ground, she shoved them into his arms. "Get dressed!"

He smiled down at her, and she couldn't help smiling back. For one instant time hung between them, breathless with the anticipation of endless future joys.

Then she heard his men shouting, heard the pounding

of machines against the earth. Heard a rush of heavy footsteps coming toward the cave, growing louder.

Sighing beneath her anxious, pleading gaze, he moved with rapid military precision, stepping into his boxers and black pants. As he pulled on his shirt, she peeked one last look at his handsome physique and marveled that she was the only woman who'd ever experienced the incredible pleasure of being in his bed. How was it possible? How was she so blessed?

She thought again of the reverent, hot, tender way he'd touched her in the night. And in the day…

"Sire? Sire!"

Kareef's chief bodyguard peered over the piled sand at the mouth of the cave, then fell to his knee in gratitude and relief. Behind him were a dozen men, geared up as if for battle. "God be praised! That blasted mare returned riderless right before the storm hit the house. We thought… We feared…"

Buttoning his ragged white shirt, Kareef stood before them, tall and proud. He looked every inch a king.

"We are safe, Faruq. Miss Kouri and I were riding when we were caught in the storm and took shelter here. Thank you for finding us." He gestured at the black stallion tied to the rock. "Please see Tayyib is cared for. He bore us well."

"Yes, sire."

"And my people? My home?"

"No injuries," the bodyguard replied. "Little damage. A great deal of sand. We brought a doctor for you just in case."

"I am unhurt. He will check Miss Kouri for injury."

Faruq glanced at her uneasily, then bowed and

backed away. She felt the other bodyguards giving her sideways glances, and her face grew hot.

"The helicopter will return us to the royal palace immediately," Kareef said. He turned to her, holding out his hand. "Miss Kouri?"

As Kareef escorted her out of the dark cave, lifting her back into the hot white sun, he smiled down at her. And all her sudden anxiety disappeared as if it had never been.

He led her to the waiting helicopter, and she smiled at him, trying to ignore the grim-faced bodyguards trailing behind. They would manage to keep their affair secret for one more day. One more precious day before Kareef would be forced to realize he had no choice but to divorce her, and they each parted to face the separate lives that fate had decreed for them.

One more day, she thought desperately. No one would be hurt by one more selfish day. A single day could feel like a lifetime.

Kareef would find a way to keep it secret. She'd never seen a secret kept at the palace, but he could find a way. He was magic. He was power.

He was king.

Kareef's shoulders were tight as he stormed through the corridors of the royal palace, scattering assistants in his wake.

Every minute of his schedule since his return to the city had been meticulously dictated by five different assistants and undersecretaries working in conjunction, overseen by the vizier. The king's duties were endless. Treaties to negotiate. False smiles under cloak of courtesy. Diplomacy. Politics. Saying one thing and meaning another. What did Kareef know of those?

He growled to himself. He was already learning far more than he'd ever wished.

He despised keeping Jasmine a secret.

She'd slept against his shoulder on the helicopter journey from the desert. He could still feel her, somehow still smell her intoxicating scent of oranges and cloves against his body, though he'd showered and changed out of his clothes and into white robes at the royal palace.

The moment he'd set foot back at the palace, he'd wanted to take her to his bedchamber; but she'd demurred, glancing at the endless secretaries and assistants waiting for him in the hallways. "Later," she'd whispered, and with a sigh, he'd let her go. He'd told himself he'd be able to cut his meetings short and return soon to her little room in the servants' wing.

That was ten hours ago. His elderly vizier, Akmal Al'Sayr, was still tearing his beard out at the days Kareef had missed. It seemed even being lost and half-presumed dead in the desert wasn't enough to excuse a monarch from his duty.

It was now twilight, and he hadn't seen Jasmine since they'd arrived at the palace. His entire day had been wasted. A day devoted to cold duty in a palace full of hidden corridors and sly whispers of gossip.

His hands tightened. He hated all this secrecy. He had to convince her to give up the marriage. He would smooth things over with Hajjar somehow. Once she agreed to call off her wedding, Kareef would be willing to divorce her. When she agreed to be his long-term mistress.

How could my parents ever hold up their heads in the street, if I let myself be branded as your whore?

The word made him flinch. No. Damn it, no! If any man dared insult her, Kareef would throw him into the Byzantine dungeon beneath the palace. He would exile him to the desert without food or water. He would—

You would kill your own subjects for speaking the truth? He heard the echo of Jasmine's whisper in the cave. *Let me go. Set me free.*

Clenching his jaw, he pushed the thought firmly from his mind. He would keep her as long as he desired her—whether that took ten years or fifty. He was young yet, only thirty-one. He would keep her for himself, and put off his own marriage as long as he could.

He quickened his pace down the hall, growling at any servant who dared to look his way.

Was Jasmine awake yet? he wondered. Was she naked beneath the sheets, with her dark hair mussed across the pillow? He felt rock-hard, aching for her. He went faster, almost breaking into a run.

"Sire, a word?"

In the hallway near the royal offices, he saw his vizier hovering in the doorway.

"Later," he ground out, not stopping.

"Of course, my king," the vizier said silkily. "I just wanted you to know I've begun negotiations for your marriage. You needn't worry about it. I will present your bride to you in a few weeks."

Stopping dead in the hallway, Kareef whirled into the reception room and closed the door behind them.

"You will arrange nothing," he said coldly. "I have no interest in marriage."

"But sire, these things take time. And you are not getting any younger…."

"I'm thirty-one!"

"After all the chaos caused by your cousin's abdication, your subjects need the comfort and security of seeing the line of succession continue. A royal wedding. A royal family." He pulled on his graying beard. "It might be difficult to find the right bride, a young virgin with the correct lineage and a perfect, unsullied reputation—"

"Why must she be a virgin?" Kareef demanded.

"So no one can ever doubt that your children are yours," he replied, sounding surprised. "You must have an undisputed heir."

Kareef clenched his jaw. "You will not negotiate a bride for me. I forbid it."

The vizier returned his look with gleaming, canny eyes. "Because your interests are elsewhere?"

Kareef looked at him narrowly, wondering how much he already knew. The vizier's spies were everywhere. He cared so obsessively about the security of the country, personal privacy meant nothing to the man. "What do you mean?"

His dark eyes affixed on Kareef. "It would be a grave mistake to insult Umar Hajjar, my king," he said quietly. "I've heard he is returning from Paris tonight."

Paris. So Kareef's suspicions had been right. Hajjar had been spending time with his French mistress.

And Kareef was expected to give up Jasmine to a man who did not even care enough to be loyal to her?

Too angry to be fair, he clenched his hands. "I have no intention of insulting Hajjar. He is my friend. He saved my life."

"Yes. Quite." The older man cleared his throat. "The royal banquet begins soon, sire. Ambassadors and foreign princes have come from all over the world to celebrate your impending coronation. You will not wish to be late."

Kareef ground his teeth. Making small talk with people he didn't care about? "I will attend in my own time."

The vizier tugged his beard. "It's just a pity you don't have your future bride on your arm for such a social event," he sighed, then brightened. "Princess Lara du Plessis is attending with her father. She is a possibility as well. She's very beautiful—"

"No marriage," Kareef barked out. His mind already on Jasmine, he turned to go.

"You will find her in the royal garden," the vizier called sourly behind him. "Where she does not deserve to be."

Kareef whirled to face him.

Jasmine was right. There were no secrets in the palace. Akmal Al'Sayr knew them all.

Except one.

He did not know Kareef was already married.

"You will call off your spies," he said grimly. "Leave her in peace."

Akmal's mouth twisted sharply downward, his lips disappearing into his long gray beard as he fell into dutiful silence.

"And find her a place at the banquet."

The vizier looked unhappier still, his slender body

drooping like a frown. But he hung his head beneath his sovereign's decree. "Yes, sire." He looked up, his beady eyes glittering. "But she can never be more to you than a mistress. The people would never accept such a woman as your wife, a woman who's had so many lovers she threw herself from a horse to lose her nameless, ill-gotten child—"

Red covered Kareef's gaze. In two strides, he'd grabbed the other man's throat.

"It was an accident," he hissed. "*An accident*. And as for her many lovers, she's had only one. Me. Do you understand, Al'Sayr? I was her lover. The only one."

The older man's eyes started to bulge before Kareef regained control. He let him go. The vizier leaned over, holding his throat and coughing.

"Never speak of her that way again," he spat out. With a growl still on his lips, Kareef whirled away in murderous fury, striding down the hall in his robes.

His heart was still pounding with rage when he found Jasmine in the royal garden in the twilight, sleeping on a cushioned seat in a shady, quiet bower. A book was folded upside down unheeded in her lap. He stopped, staring down at her, marveling again at her beauty.

She slept peacefully, like a child. The wind blew softly through the trees, rattling the leaves, brushing loose tendrils of dark hair across her face. She was wearing a fitted black sweater over a high-necked white shirt and a long black skirt. And below that—red canvas sneakers.

Her lovely face was bare of makeup, and beautiful in its natural simplicity. Modest, simple, like a maid. She looked the part of a perfect wife and mother—the perfect heart of any man's home. *Of his home.*

He took a deep breath, calming down beneath the influence of her sweet purity, of her innocence. He smiled down at her. Then his gaze fell upon her hand, and he saw she still wore Hajjar's diamond upon her finger.

Jasmine's dark brown eyes fluttered open. A smile lit up her face when she saw him. Her smile struck through his soul.

"Kareef." The sweet lilt of her voice washed over him like a wave of water. "Oh, how I've missed you today!"

He sat next to her, taking her hands in his own. "I thought the day would never end."

"And once again, you've caught me in the royal garden." Her expression became bashful, apologetic. "Where I should not be."

"The garden is yours," he said roughly. "You have the right."

She tried to smile at him, but her expression faltered. She looked down at her hand, twisting the ring on her finger. "For now."

A spasm of unexpected jealousy went through him as he looked at that ring, the physical mark of another man's ownership. "Take that off."

She looked at him in surprise. "Why?"

"Take it off."

"No."

"You're not going to marry him tomorrow."

Her expression became mutinous. "I am." She rose to her feet. "And if you can't accept that—"

"We won't talk about it now, then." He caught her wrist. "Just come to the royal banquet with me tonight."

She looked down at his hand on her wrist.

"This is how we would be discreet?" she said. "Beside each other at the banquet, as lovers for all the world to see?" She shook her head. He saw tears in her eyes. "Admit I was right," she whispered. "The palace separates us already. Let's end this cleanly. We must part."

He looked at her with a heavy heart. How could he change her mind, when he himself could feel the truth of her words?

But taking a deep breath, he shook his head. "One more night."

"It won't change anything."

"Attend the banquet with me. Give me one last chance to change your mind, to convince you not to marry him. One last night." He set his jaw. "Then, if you still wish to wed him—I will say farewell."

He watched her face as her expression struggled visibly between desire and pain. "You will divorce me?"

"Yes."

"On your honor?"

"Yes," he bit out.

She gave him a slow nod. "Very well." She reached out to caress his cheek, then hesitated. She glanced wryly at her red high-top sneakers. "I will go get dressed." She bowed her head, then looked up. Tears glistened in her eyes. "Until tonight, my king."

A half hour later, Kareef arrived alone to thunderous applause at the grand ballroom. Five hundred illustrious guests clamored for his attention, clamored for his gaze—and he still hadn't thought of a way to convince Jasmine to remain his mistress. Because there wasn't a solution.

Jasmine wanted respectability. She wanted a family of her own. She wanted children.

As king, what could he offer her—except disgrace?

Greeting his honored guests, Kareef walked to the end of the long table, looking for one beautiful face. Where was she? Where had the vizier placed her? Without her calming presence, he felt like a trapped tiger in a cage, half-mad in captivity. He prayed to find her beside him at the table.

But when he reached his place, he stopped.

Seated on his left he saw the elderly king of a neighboring nation.

Seated on his right was a beautiful blonde of no more than eighteen, bedecked in diamonds and giggling behind her hand as she stared up at him with big blue eyes. He instantly knew who she must be: Princess Lara du Plessis.

Silently cursing his vizier, Kareef sat down. His hands clenched on the fine linen tablecloth of the table. He stared dismally at his plate setting of 24-karat gold-patterned china and crystal stemware filled with champagne. Where was Jasmine?

As the meal was served, the elderly king on his left complained at length about some unfair customs tax between Qusay and his own country, and it was all Kareef could do to keep from turning his ceremonial dagger on himself, like a wolf chewing off his own paw to escape a trap.

Then he felt the prickles rise on the back of his neck. And he looked up.

Jasmine looked at him from the other side of the ballroom, as far away as she could possibly be. She'd been seated beside some plain woman dressed in brown and the fat, balding secretary of the Minister of the Treasury. No doubt a location that the vizier had arranged for her personally.

She tried to give him an encouraging smile, but her eyes were sad. The shadows of the darkening ballroom beneath the candlelit chandeliers made everyone else disappear.

She was so beautiful. And so far away.

His heart turned over in his chest. Was this all it was to be, then? Was this all he could offer her? To be his secret mistress, fit only for clandestine trysts in his bedroom—instead of be the honored companion by his side?

Kareef ate quickly and spoke in monosyllables to the elderly king and the giggling young princess when they forced a direct question upon him. The instant the musicians and fire dancers arrived in the ballroom, signaling the end of the banquet, the candles were put out to highlight the magic of the performance.

Kareef threw his linen napkin on his plate and went to her.

The shadows were dark and deep as he made his way through the ballroom. All the audience was mesmerized by the intricacies of a dance with flames and swords, set to the haunting melody of the *jowza* and *santur*. Kareef was invisible in the darkness. He passed many whispered conversations that he knew would never be spoken before the king.

"…Jasmine Kouri," he heard a woman hiss, and in spite of himself, he slowed to listen. "Spending every day with him at the palace—and nights, too, I wager.

The king's a good, honorable man but when a woman is so determined to spread her legs…"

"And her an engaged woman!" came the spiteful reply. "She's made a fool out of Umar Hajjar for wanting to marry her. You remember that scandal when she was young? She was bad from the start."

"She'll get her comeuppance. Wait and see…."

Hands clenched, Kareef whirled to see who was speaking, but the women's voices faded and blended into the rest of the crowd. He saw only moving shadows.

Oh God, give him an honest fight! A fight where he could face his enemy—not the whisper of spiteful gossips in the dark!

He was still trembling with fury when he reached the lower tables of the ballroom. He whispered Jasmine's name silently. He craved her touch, yearned to have her in his arms. He yearned to keep her safe, to somehow give her shelter from the cruel words.

But when he reached for her chair, it was empty.

The instant the musicians entered the ballroom with their guitars, dulcimers and flutes in an eerie, haunting accompaniment to dancing swords of fire in the abruptly darkened ballroom, Jasmine bolted from her seat.

The banquet had been hell. She'd heard whispers and caught stares in her direction—some curious, some envious, a few hateful. It was clear that in spite of the fact that she and Kareef had neither kissed nor slept in the same bed since they'd returned to the palace, everyone already believed she was his lover. And they blamed her—*only her*—for that sin.

On her right side at the table, a fat, balding man had

leered at her throughout the meal. On her left, a plain woman had stiffened in her mousy brown suit and pointedly ignored her for a solid hour.

Jasmine had watched Kareef across the ballroom. He was clearly adored and praised by his subjects, and he accepted their attention carelessly, as his due.

Kareef didn't need her in his life, whatever he might say. He was surrounded by people begging for his attention, including the virginal blonde princess seated beside him. She was the type of woman he no doubt would marry—very soon.

She'd fled as soon as the ballroom went dark. She'd been desperate to escape before anyone could see her tears. But as soon as she was in the hallway, she felt a hand on her shoulder and whirled around, her hands tightened into fists.

Then her hands grew lax. Her body went numb.

"Father," she whispered. "What are you doing here?"

Yazid Kouri seemed to have aged in just the last few days, his once-powerful frame grown stooped and thin. He looked her over from her careful chignon to the black formal dress she'd borrowed from her old friend Sera for the occasion.

He gave a harsh laugh. "Why did you come back here?"

"You know why—"

"I thought you'd at last become a respectable, dutiful girl." He shook his head, his black eyes suspiciously bright. "Why would you agree to marry a respectable man, only to betray him with the king before you have even spoken your vows?"

She shook her head. "You don't understand!"

"Tell me you've never lain with the king," he said. "Tell me it's just an ugly rumor, and I'll believe you."

Blinking fast, she looked away. Her father's disappointment hurt her so badly she could hardly bear it. "I've betrayed no one except myself. There is no shame if I am with the king, not when he…not when we…"

Not when we're married. But the words caught at her throat. She couldn't reveal their secret. The king's word of honor was admired around the world. How could she reveal that he'd hidden such a secret for thirteen years?

As a girl, she'd remained silent to protect him.

As a woman, she still would.

"You see nothing wrong in sleeping with a man who is not your husband?" her father continued, his voice sodden with grief. "That sort of behavior might be acceptable in the modern world, but not in our family. Your sister needs you. Marry Umar. Return to New York with your new husband and family. Help Nima raise her child!"

Jasmine's jaw dropped. "You've spoken to her?"

"She called us two hours ago." He looked away, his jaw clenching. "She says she doesn't know how to be a mother. She's threatening to give the child to strangers when it's born! She's scared. She's so young."

Fury suddenly raced through Jasmine, fury she could not control. She raised her head.

"Just as I was!" she cried. "I was sixteen when you threw me out of our family, out of our country!"

"I was angry," he whispered. Tears filled his bleary eyes. "I had different expectations of you, Jasmine. You were my eldest. You had such intelligence, such strength. I took so much pride in you. Then…it all fell apart."

Her heart turned over in her chest.

"Go back to New York as a married woman. Steady Nima with your strength." His eyes glistened with unshed tears. "Tomorrow, I will be in Qais, expecting to see a wedding."

Turning to leave, he stopped when he saw Kareef standing behind them, his body tense in the ceremonial white robes.

Her father's face went almost purple. Distraught, he raised his fists against the much taller, stronger man. "I should kill you for the way you've shamed my daughter!"

Kareef didn't move. He didn't flinch. He just stood there, waiting to accept the blow.

Her father dropped his fists. Tears streaked down his wrinkled face.

"You're no king," he said hoarsely, his voice shaking with grief. "You're not even a man."

Turning on his heel, he stumbled down the palace hallway.

Jasmine watched him. When he was gone, she crumpled. Kareef pulled her into his arms and held her fast as she cried.

Softly stroking her head, he looked down at her, cupping her face with his hands. His eyes were deep and dark as he wiped the tears from her cheeks with his thumbs. He took a deep breath. Then his shoulders fell in resignation.

"Come with me," he whispered.

In the ballroom behind them, she could still hear the eerie music and shouts of the performers behind the closed doors. But Kareef led her down the dark hallway, passing several servants who pretended not to notice, who pretended not to see that the king had left his own banquet with a woman who belonged to another.

Kareef took her down the hallway into the east wing, into his bedchamber. Closing the door behind them, he set her down on the enormous bed.

Sitting on the bed beside her, he leaned over and kissed her. Tears streamed unchecked down her face as she kissed him back with all her heart. Everything she felt for him, all the tenderness of a young girl's dreams and the fire of a woman's desire, came through in her kiss.

His enormous gilded bedroom was dark. The balcony window was open, and a hot desert wind blew in from the garden, along with the noise, sudden explosions of laughter and applause from the ballroom on the floor below. But they were a world apart.

Gently, tenderly, he lay her back against his bed and made love to her one last time. The ecstasy of her body was as sharp as the pain in her heart.

I love you, her soul cried. *I love you*. But she knew her love changed nothing.

When he brought her to aching, gasping fulfillment, she wept. For a moment, he held her tightly against his chest, in his arms, as if he never wanted to let her go.

Then he slowly rose from the bed. He put on his clothes. Without looking at her, he went to an antique, jeweled chest beside the bookshelf. He twisted a key in the lock and opened it. Reaching inside, he pulled something out and returned to where she sat, clothed and numb on the bed.

He held out her emerald necklace, dangling it from his hand. She stared at the green facets of the stone, without moving.

He took her hand and placed the emerald in her palm, folding her fingers over the gold chain.

She heard the ragged gasp of his breath. Then his posture became hard as granite. He placed his hand over hers. When he spoke, his voice was deep and cold, echoing in the cavernous royal bedchamber.

"Jasmine, I divorce you."

CHAPTER NINE

THE next morning, Jasmine stepped out of the helicopter, craning her neck to stare up at the modern, gleaming racetrack that split the desert flatlands from the wide loneliness of the blue sky.

Qais. The desert she loved. But now the freedom had a sting. Horizons stretched out around her, mocking her as she stood dressed from head-to-toe in clothes chosen for her by someone else.

Her clothes had finally arrived from Paris, and she was now dressed to please her future husband, in a belted red silk dress from Christian Dior, Christian Louboutin black heels, a black vintage Kelly bag and a wide-brimmed black-and-white hat. Her beautiful designer clothes felt like a costume from the 1950s, stylish and severe.

She no longer had freedom here. Not even in the clothes she wore.

Jasmine looked up at the glass stadium that Kareef and Umar had built together. It wasn't the only thing the two men would soon share. When the Qais Cup was over, her wedding would begin.

Kareef followed her with the rest of his bodyguards

and assistants. She saw him hesitate, then grimly push forward. What more was there to say?

He'd already given the bride away.

Jasmine stared at his tense, muscular back as he walked ahead of her. She memorized the turn of his head, the line of his jaw. The shape of his supremely masculine body as he walked in his white robes.

Unwillingly, she remembered the feel of his naked body against her own. The sweet satisfied ache of pain as he possessed her, the way her lips felt bruised from his kiss, her inner thighs scratched from the sandpaper-roughness of his jaw. The memory made her body tighten with a rush of heat, even as her soul shook with the anguish of loss.

With a deep breath, she forced herself to look up.

Rising from the desert, the glass stadium competed with the blinding sun for brilliance. But even the desert sun couldn't burn away the taste of Kareef, the exotic scent of his skin. It couldn't burn away the memory of his hard body covering hers. Or the look in his blue eyes last night when he'd spoken the words to divorce her.

"My dear." Umar stepped forward from a private side door of the stadium and leaned forward to kiss her cheek gently. "I am so glad to see you at last."

In spite of his words, he looked pale. As he pulled away from her, she made no move to kiss him back, no attempt to even smile. "Where have you been, Umar?"

Umar's pale cheeks turned pink. "France," he muttered. "There was a family emergency. With Léa."

"With your nanny?" Jasmine said. "Is everything all right?"

"Fine. Fine," he said with an uneven smile. He

seemed strangely nervous and jittery compared to the urbane, sophisticated man she knew.

Turning away, he started walking, practically running toward the door, though propriety demanded that the king should have gone first. They had to hurry to keep up with him, or else be left behind.

"And that's all you have to say to me?" she demanded.

"The race is about to start." Umar glanced back at her, his nose wrinkling like a rabbit's before he sighed. "When it's over, we'll talk."

Jasmine stared at him. Had he heard the rumors about her and Kareef being lovers? Did he no longer wish to marry her?

Was he going to abandon her at the altar, to her family's eternal shame?

"Wait," she choked out. "Whatever you've heard, I can explain—"

"Later." Umar hurried toward the door. "Your family is already here. I had them seated in a place not too far from the royal box, in a place of honor." He paused. "I'll be sitting with my children in the box next to yours. You're in the royal box with the king."

So he'd heard!

"Wait!" she cried. "You don't understand!"

Kareef came up behind her. "Afraid to be alone with me?" he said in a low voice.

She glanced back at him, and trembled at the darkness in his blue eyes. She swallowed, fighting back tears. This was hard. So much harder than she'd thought it would be!

"Is my arrangement acceptable, my king?" Umar asked Kareef with a bow of his head.

Kareef answered with a single hard nod, then looked back at Jasmine with glittering eyes.

Divorced. They were divorced. But that hadn't changed her feelings. It didn't keep her body from crying out for his touch. The divorce changed nothing.

"Thank you, sire." Umar ducked inside the grandstand.

She felt Kareef's fierce blue gaze upon her like the merciless desert sun, charring her soul, turning it to dust. He glowered, then walked past her.

Lifting her chin, she put one hand on her head, balancing her wide-brimmed hat as she followed him through the private door and up the stairs. They passed through an enclosed, air-conditioned private room with a one-way mirror overlooking the track, and finally came out into the open-air royal box.

Kareef went outside first.

When he was visible to the crowds in the stadium, forty thousand people rose to their feet, screaming his name.

He raised his hand to them.

The screaming intensified.

Coming out into the royal box behind him, Jasmine pressed her hand against her belly, holding her black handbag against her body like a shield against the roar of the crowd.

She looked at his beautiful, savage face. Saw the lines of strength and wisdom at his eyes, saw the powerful jut of his jawline. Honor was the heart of who he was.

She'd done the right thing, no matter how it killed her.

She'd set him free to be the king he was born to be.

Kareef finally sat down and she sank into the chair beside him. She was aware of him at every moment but didn't look in his direction. Instead, she pressed her fingers against her wide-brimmed hat, blocking the sun from her eyes as she stared out at the racetrack.

Thousands of people stared back at her. Sitting beside the handsome, powerful young king, Jasmine knew she must appear to be very fortunate. Even though some of the older women whispered maliciously behind their hands, she could see their modern daughters looking at her belted, form-fitting red silk dress and handbag with envy. Looking at her expensive, pretty clothes and the handsome, powerful man beside her, they were no doubt thinking a lost reputation would be a small price to pay for such a glamorous life.

If only they knew what Jasmine really felt like on the inside. The truth was that she wished she had a spoon, so she could cut her heart out with it.

Beautiful clothes, wealth, attention and power— none of that mattered. Not when she couldn't have the man she loved.

"Did you sleep well?" Kareef said in a low voice beside her.

"Yes," she lied over the lump in her throat, turning away as she fought back tears. "Very well."

The gunshot sounded the start of the race, and the horses bolted from the gates.

She felt the hot burn of Kareef's gaze on her. Felt it by the way her neck prickled. By the way her nipples tightened and her breasts became heavy. She fanned herself with a program, sweating from a blast of heat that had nothing to do with the white desert sun above the grandstand.

In the next box over, she could see Umar sitting with his four young sons. The two-year-old baby was snuggled contentedly in the lap of the French nanny, Léa, who while not strictly pretty, had a sweet look to her plump face. She was only a few years older than Jasmine. Umar sat back in his chair until the horses pounded by their seats in a loud torrent of thundering hooves, and he rose to his feet, shouting at his horse in a mixture of cursing and praise.

The four boys were all adorable, Jasmine thought. She would soon be their stepmother. But even that thought didn't cheer her as it used to. None of the children wanted her. They already seemed to have a mother—Léa.

As the horses neared the finish line, Umar gripped the railing, pumping his fist in the air as he watched. "Go! Go, damn you!"

Jasmine saw her mother and father sitting in a different section with her sisters, along with her sisters' husbands and children. She hesitantly lifted her hand in greeting at her father.

Her father scowled at her in the royal box. He coldly turned his head away.

Jasmine set her shoulders. It didn't matter, she told herself over the lump in her throat. Once she was married—if Umar still married her—her father would finally be proud of her. She would do the right thing. Even if it killed her.

She heard Umar shout with delight, heard him clap his hands. His horse had won. Ruffling the hair of one of his older sons, he rushed off to accept his prize, his children following behind with the nanny. Watching them, Jasmine felt more like an outsider than ever.

She rose to her feet and went to the front of the royal box. She watched Umar walking out onto the racetrack, waving to the crowd as he crossed the grass.

"It means nothing to you, does it," Kareef said behind her in a low voice, "that you'll give your body to him tonight, when you were in my bed only yesterday?"

She pretended to smile down at Umar on the racetrack as he exuberantly accepted flowers, patting his horse's nose and shaking his jockey's hand. "We are divorced," she said, fighting to keep her voice even. "You mean nothing to me."

"Don't marry him, Jasmine." His voice was hoarse and deep. She heard him rise from his chair. "Don't."

She saw her fiancé waving and smiling. He lifted his two-year-old son on his shoulder, and the crowd roared their approval.

She felt Kareef come up behind her, close enough to touch. She didn't turn around. She couldn't. The cheers of the crowd became deafening white noise, like static. Until all Jasmine could hear was the pounding of her own heart and the rush of blood in her ears.

She felt Kareef slowly pull off her wide-brimmed hat. The back of her neck was washed in the warmth of his breath. Her body tightened from her scalp to her breasts, and a sweet agonizing tension coiled low and deep inside her.

"Stay with me," Kareef said in a low voice. "Not because you're bound to me, but because it's your free choice. Be my mistress."

The king's mistress.

For that kind of joy, Jasmine would have willingly sacrificed anything. Except one thing. Her gaze fell upon her family.

She squeezed her eyes closed. She'd thought she'd known pain before, but this was more than she could bear. With an intake of breath, she whirled around in his arms. Ripping the hat out of his grasp, she held it against her handbag as she backed away. "I can't."

"Jasmine—"

"Go back to the palace, Kareef," she choked out. "Don't stay for my wedding. It kills me to have you so close—don't you see you're killing me?"

She turned and rushed up the steps toward the air-conditioned private room, disappearing behind the door.

Kareef caught up with her almost instantly on the other side of the mirrored window. Grabbing her, he pushed her roughly against the wall. Both hat and handbag dropped hard on the floor. She struggled, but his hands wrapped around her wrists, holding her fast. She couldn't run. She couldn't escape. She couldn't resist.

She braced for a savage plundering of her lips. She waited for him to crush her. Instead, he did something far worse. He lowered his mouth to hers in a kiss far more brutal than any mere force could ever be.

He kissed her…as if he loved her.

Kareef moved his hands over Jasmine's red silk dress, savoring the feel of her curvaceous body in his arms. Relief filled him that she was back where she belonged. Desire sizzled through his veins like a drug as he tasted the exquisite sweetness of her lips.

He'd thought he'd almost lost her. He'd divorced her, as he'd given his word of honor to do. But he still wanted her. He wanted her to choose to be with him, of her own free will. To choose him over all other men, no matter how inconvenient or difficult their love might be.

Didn't she realize that they'd already lost too many years of their lives apart?

She belonged to him. As he belonged to her.

He cupped her breasts through her dress, stroking her shoulders, her swanlike neck. He kissed her skin, biting almost hard enough to bruise. He wanted to mark his possession, to remove any memory of another man's claim on her. *To rip that damned diamond off her left hand.*

"You belong to me," he growled. "Say it."

Her beautiful chocolate-brown eyes gleamed and shimmered, sliding over him with the sensuality of a hot desert night. His body's memory of making love to her so many times, so urgently, roared through him like a blaze. His hands tightened.

"I belong to you," she whispered with an intake of breath. "But Kareef, you must know that we—"

He stopped her with a hard kiss. He felt her tremble beneath him as he stroked her body through the red silk. He wrapped his hands in her lustrous dark hair, amid chestnut streaks like woven gold in the daylight.

They belonged together. Now, he would let the whole world know it. He would no longer hide his love for Jasmine in the shadows.

His love.

Oh my God. He loved her.

He didn't just desire Jasmine. He didn't just wish to spend his every moment with her.

He loved her. He'd never stopped loving her. It was why he'd never once felt tempted by the endless succession of women who'd tried to throw themselves into his bed. His body, his heart, were for one woman only.

Jasmine.

Even if it cost him his crown. Even if it cost him his life. He would have them together. In the open. *In the sun.*

Cupping her face, he kissed her tenderly, kissing her closed eyelids, her cheeks, her mouth. A sigh escaped her lips as she swayed in his arms, turning her face toward his.

He wrapped her left hand in his own, pressing it up against his heart as he looked down at her. "I'll tell Hajjar the wedding is off."

Smiling, he grasped the enormous diamond ring and started to draw it off her finger.

But she closed her hand into a fist. He stared at her in exasperation.

"Jasmine," he demanded.

Her face was blank of expression as she shook her head.

"You will be my honored mistress," he said, his brow furrowed. "My queen in all but name. There will be no more sneaking in the shadows, no shame for your family. I will treat you as the highest lady in the land, and the whole country will follow my lead."

"And Umar?"

"He will forgive us."

"And you?" She slowly looked up at him. "When you take your bride, Qusay's queen? What will become of me then?"

He set his jaw. The thought made him sick.

"Perhaps I will die a bachelor," he growled.

"But you need an heir," she whispered.

He shrugged, a casual gesture that belied the repressed emotion in his eyes. "My brothers' children can inherit," he said lightly. "Or their grandchildren. I intend to live a very long life."

"But your brothers are not even married. What makes you think they ever will be?"

He felt brief uncertainty, which swiftly changed to anger and impatience. "They will."

"They don't even care enough about Qusay to live here. Do you think Rafiq would give up his billion-dollar business empire to come back from Australia and rule? And from what I've heard, Tahir is squandering his life away on the international party circuit—"

"People can change—"

"Are you willing to risk the throne of Qusay on that? To place that kind of burden on your younger brothers?" She shook her head desperately. "Even if they do someday have children or grandchildren... those grandchildren will know nothing of Qusay. You think our people would tolerate being ruled by someone ignorant of our languages, our customs?"

His jaw clenched as he looked away. When he looked back at her, his voice was full of agony he no longer tried to hide.

"Is there no chance you could get pregnant, Jasmine?" he said hoarsely. "Not even a small chance? We could see the best fertility specialist in the world, spare no expense, do whatever it took for you to bear my child—"

"No," she said brutally. "I've visited some of the top obstetricians in Manhattan. I got second and third opinions. I can never get pregnant." A sob rose to her lips. "I won't destroy my family by becoming your mistress." She wiped her eyes, lifting her chin. "I deserve more than that. And so do you," she whispered.

He grabbed her shoulders savagely.

"I've waited for you for thirteen years. I'm not going to lose you again." His hands tightened on her painfully. "Even if the whole world goes down in flames for it. I'm not going to let you go."

She looked up at him, so impossibly beautiful. Unreachable.

Behind her, the bright flowers and garish red-and-gilt of the private room seemed flat, as if covered by dark mist. Outside the mirrored window, the green grass and brown horses and colorful shirts of the jockeys seemed to fade to black as Jasmine pushed away from him coldly, kneeling to pick up her hat and purse from the carpet.

"Marry another," she said in a low voice, not looking at him. "Be the king you were born to be."

He stared at her. "Is it so easy for you to thrust me into the arms of another?"

She sucked in her breath. Her eyes were stricken.

"No," she choked out. "I hate the woman you'll marry. Whoever she might be."

"And I'll hate any man who has you in his bed. Even the friend who saved my life." He looked down at her, his jaw hard. "You won't be my mistress. So there is only one answer. You will marry me."

Her jaw dropped. "What?"

"Marry me. *You* must be my queen, Jasmine. Only you."

Her eyes were huge. Then she seemed to shudder, blinking her eyes as if closing a door in her heart.

"It cannot be. You need an heir. If you married me—whatever you might think—you would be forced to abdicate."

"I have the right to choose my own bride—"

"No," she cut him off harshly. "You don't."

"But Jasmine…" he started, then stopped. He'd offered her everything. His kingdom. His name. He'd offered her everything he had, and she'd refused.

But he hadn't offered her everything. There was one risk he hadn't taken.

"But you have to marry me, Jasmine," he said. "You have to be my wife, because I…" He took a deep breath and looked straight into her eyes. "I love you."

Her eyes widened. He saw her tremble. Then slowly, ruthlessly, she squared her shoulders.

"Then you're a fool," she said evenly. "I pity you with all my heart."

With a growl, he started toward her. "But you love me," he said. "Tell the truth. You love me, as I love you!"

She held up her hand.

"The truth is that I want what you cannot give me." Her voice was cold as ice, like a sharp icicle through his heart. "Marrying Umar might be my only chance to ever have children." Her eyes narrowed as she delivered the killing blow. "You took away my chance to be a mother, Kareef," she whispered. "You took away my chance to ever have a child."

It was his greatest grief. His greatest fear. The guilty thought he'd whispered silently around the desert fire by night. Only this was a thousand times worse, since the accusation fell from the lips of the woman he loved.

His agonized blue eyes were focused on her. He took a single stumbling step backward, bumping a nearby silver champagne bucket on a table. It crashed to the floor in an explosion of ice. The bottle rolled against the wall, scattering ice and champagne across the carpet.

But he didn't notice. Pain racked his body, ripping him into little pieces more completely and ruthlessly than any sandstorm.

You took away my chance to ever have a child.

Pain and grief poured through him, burning like lava.

She'd told him it had been an accident. She'd told him he was forgiven.

Lies—all lies!

Suddenly, he could not contain the rage and grief inside his own body. Savagely, he turned and smashed a hole in a nearby wall. She flinched back, gasping.

"Teach me how to feel nothing, like you," he said in a low voice. "I'm tired of having a heart. From the moment I loved you, it has never stopped breaking."

Walking away from her, he paused in the doorway without looking back. He didn't want her to see his face. When he spoke, his voice was choked with grief.

"Goodbye, Jasmine," he said, leaning his head against the door as he closed his eyes. "I wish you a life filled with every happiness."

And he left her.

CHAPTER TEN

AN HOUR later, Jasmine looked blankly at her own image in the large gilded mirror of the late Mrs. Hajjar's pink bedroom.

"Oh, my daughter," her father said tenderly as he pulled the veil over her head. "You're the most beautiful bride I've ever seen."

"So beautiful," her plump, gray-haired mother agreed, beaming at her. "I'll go tell them you're ready."

Jasmine stared at herself in the mirror. The round window behind her lit up her white veil with afternoon sunlight, leaving her face in shadow. She was having trouble breathing and could barely move, laced into a tight corset, locked into a wide hoop skirt beneath the layers of tulle.

Umar had ordered every component of this gown for her, even her underwear, from a Paris couture house six months before she'd agreed to be his bride. She looked at the mirror. The perfect gilded princess for this garish palace.

She could see the desert through the window behind her. She could almost imagine, in a far distance, a low-slung ranch house of brown wood, with trees and simply tended flowers beside a swimming pool of endless blue, and a loggia where she'd once held the man she loved, naked against her body.

Here in the desert, the harsh sun burned away all the lies.

Except for one.

The lie Jasmine had told to drive Kareef away.

Staring at the perfect bride in the mirror, she felt dizzy from the frantic beat of her heart.

Kareef had told her he'd loved her.

And she'd tossed his love back in his face!

I had no choice, she told herself as her knees shook beneath her. *I had no choice! He asked to marry me. He would have been forced to abdicate the throne for me!*

To push him away, she'd conjured the most cruel spell, the most vicious accusation she could imagine to drive him away from her. She'd used his own grief and guilt against him.

It made her sick inside. No matter how pure her motives, she knew she'd committed the deepest betrayal of the heart. And if she married Umar today, she would be committing suicide of the soul.

And suddenly, she knew she couldn't do it.

She could not marry a man she did not love.

For any reason.

"Where is Umar?" she whispered, pressing her hands against her tightly corseted waist, struggling for breath. "He said we would talk before the wedding. Please find him."

"I don't think that's such a good idea—" her father began ponderously.

"We'll find him," her mother said, giving her husband a sharp look. She smiled at Jasmine. "Don't worry."

"Wait." She grabbed her mother's wrist. A lump rose in her throat at the sudden fear that Jasmine would never see her again.

"Why Jasmine," her mother said softly, stroking her hair though the veil as if she were still a little girl. "What's wrong?"

Would they forgive her for calling off the wedding? Would they ever forgive her?

She would pray they would. She'd do everything she could to help her sister. She'd do everything she could to show her family she loved them.

But not sacrifice her soul.

"Mother," Jasmine said, fighting back tears, "I know I haven't always made you proud but…" Sniffling beneath her elegant veil, she looked from her mother to her father, then shook her head. "I love you both so much."

"And we've always loved you, Jasmine," her mother said, squeezing Jasmine's hand. "We always will."

"Come," her father said gruffly, pulling his wife away. "Let us leave Jasmine in peace."

Her mother's hand slipped away. The door shut softly.

With a deep breath, Jasmine opened her eyes in the flowery pink bedroom designed by Umar's dead wife. Jasmine saw moving rainbows against the wallpaper. She looked down to see the enormous diamond on her hand with its endless reflecting facets. She pulled the ring off her finger.

The stone was so cold, she thought, looking down at it in her palm. So hard. So dead.

Teach me how to feel nothing, like you. I'm tired of having a heart. From the moment I loved you, it has never stopped breaking.

Kareef had already left Qais, she'd heard, returning to the city on his helicopter. Tomorrow morning, he would be crowned king—alone.

Jasmine had finally gotten what she wanted. She'd finally pushed him away.

The ring fell from her lifeless hands. Jasmine sank to the floor, enshrouded by layers of white tulle as she fell forward into the voluminous white skirts. Her head hung down as her whole body was racked with sobs of grief.

"Oh my God," she heard Umar say in the doorway. "Someone told you."

"I'm sorry," she whispered, covering her veiled face with her hands. "I'm so sorry…."

She felt Umar's arms around her. "I'm the one who's sorry," he said. "I should have told you days ago."

Staring up at him, she said, "Told me what?"

"I've been courting you for so long, but you pushed me away, and she was right there, warm and loving. She was never the type of woman I thought I would take for a bride. She has no money, no connections, no particular beauty." Shaking his head, he stared at the floor. "In the middle of our engagement party, she called me. She said she thought she might be pregnant."

"Pregnant," Jasmine breathed. "Who? Who are you talking about?"

"Léa," he whispered. He shook his head. "I never should have allowed my courtship of you to continue while I was sleeping with another woman. I told myself Léa didn't count. She was a servant. But my children love her, and she's pregnant with my child. I must marry her." He pressed his hands over hers, his voice pleading for understanding. "I *want* to marry her. Though she is nothing like the bride I imagined…I think I could love her." He pressed her hands to his forehead as he bowed his head. "Forgive me," he said humbly.

"There's nothing to forgive," she said. A half-hysterical laugh burbled to her lips. "Because I myself…"

He gave her a sideways glance. "You and the king?" He smiled. "Gossip that rich travels swiftly, even to Brittany, where I was getting permission from Léa's father to marry her."

Umar had four children already, and would soon have a new baby. Shaking her head, Jasmine stared at the carpet. In the shifting patterns of colored light from the round window, she could imagine a meadow of flowers, hear a child's laughter. She looked up into his face. "I wish you every happiness," she said softly. "You and your precious little ones."

He kissed her hand in gratitude. "You are too good," he whispered.

She stared at the patterns of sunlight on the floor. Good? She was far from good. Picking up the ring, she handed it to him.

"What will you do?" he asked.

She took a deep breath. "Go back to New York. Run my business. Help my sister however she needs me."

"And the king?"

She shook her head. "His duty lies elsewhere."

"Are you sure?"

Trembling, she rose to her feet. "He must marry a woman who can give him children."

"Sometimes, Jasmine," Umar said, looking at her quietly, "you must put aside the person everyone wants you to be—to become the person you were born to be."

She stared at him.

For years, Jasmine had lived alone in New York, working to build her investment portfolio. She'd focused on the past and the future, but never the present.

Now the past was done. The future was unknowable. But she was only twenty-nine years old. There could be a life for her back in New York, if she chose to create one. She could make her sterile Park Avenue apartment a comfortable home. She could start with a fresh clean slate.

"Is there anything I can do for you, Jasmine?" he asked. "Perhaps explain to your father?"

She gave a deep, shaky laugh. "That's an idea," she said wryly, then shook her head. "There is one thing. You have that private plane…."

"Done."

She pulled the white veil off her head, dropping it to the floor in a shimmering cascade of translucent light.

"I cannot allow Kareef to sacrifice himself for me. But there is one thing I can do." She glanced out the round window, thinking of the ranch house, far across the unseen desert. She straightened. "I can watch him become a king. And before I leave Qusay, I can take back a lie. I can tell him…" She took a deep breath. "I can tell him the truth."

Kareef looked around the royal bedchamber in the bright sunlight.

His coronation day.

His enormous bedroom was richly appointed, lavishly decorated and big enough for the ten servants that usually insisted on waiting on him. This morning, he'd thrown them all out. He would dress for his coronation—alone.

Slowly, he picked up the ceremonial sword with emeralds on the scabbard and wrapped the belt around his white robes. So much had changed in the last week. And yet nothing had changed.

He was king.

He was alone.

And he felt nothing.

He had dim memories of flying back from the desert last night after the Qais Cup. He was fairly sure he'd spent the evening making small talk with foreign dignitaries. But he could not recall any conversation or whom he'd spoken with. When he tried to think of last night all he could recall was the image of Jasmine's pale expression, the way she'd flinched when he'd punched the hole in the wall.

You took away my chance to ever have a child.

Punching the wall, he'd been trying to rid himself of the pain. In a way, it had worked. His hand still felt numb. Just like the rest of him.

He'd offered Jasmine everything. His name. His throne. His love. And she'd still refused him.

You're a fool. I pity you with all my heart.

The servants waiting outside his bedchamber door followed him in a line as he went down to the breakfast room for his final meal before the formal coronation.

Final meal, he thought dully. *The condemned man ate a hearty breakfast.*

He'd loved her. He loved her still. But he could not have her.

"Ah, sire!" the vizier said brightly as he entered the room. "Good morning! A fine joyful day, sunny and perfect for the first official day of your reign. Now that you are free of…er…entanglements, perhaps after the coronation, I might have your permission to begin the process of seeking a royal bride?"

Kareef looked up at him wearily at the word *entanglements*. Akmal Al'Sayr gave a single discreet grimace. The man had somehow discovered already that Jasmine had thrown him over, and he was so damn happy about it. It made Kareef grind his teeth.

"Fine," he bit out. If Jasmine could move on, then so could he. He'd lived without love before. He could do it again.

Duty was all he had left. Cold, endless duty.

"Perfect, sire! I have several lovely princesses to choose from."

"Choose whomever you like," Kareef said heavily.

"I know the perfect bride. She's already here to attend the coronation. I will speak with her family immediately, and if they agree, we will begin negotiations later this afternoon." He paused. "Unless you'd care to meet the girl first?"

"I don't need to meet her," he said flatly. "Just make sure she understands this is a political marriage, nothing more."

"Of course, sire. I will tell her." Akmal paused delicately. "Although of course there must be children.…"

Kareef looked down at his plate and saw that it was empty. Somehow, without tasting any of his food, he'd gotten it all down. The thought made him grimly glad. He would survive. At least his body would, and that was all that was required, wasn't it?

"Ready?" His brother Rafiq entered the breakfast room.

"Is Tahir here?"

"No sign of him."

"Right." Why was he not surprised? Of course his youngest brother had changed his mind about coming home, promise or no promise. Kareef thought of his own optimism and joy a few days ago and felt like the exact same fool Jasmine claimed him to be.

Rising slowly to his feet, Kareef followed his brother down the long hall. But as he went outside the door and into the courtyard overlooking the cliffs above the Mediterranean, he heard someone scream his name. One sweet voice above the rest. A ghost from a long-forgotten dream.

But he kept walking. He didn't even turn his head.

Then Kareef heard it again. He stopped.

"Did you hear that?"

"I heard nothing," the vizier said nervously, then tried to sweep them forward. "This way, if you please, sire. You don't wish to be late.…"

Kareef took another few steps. Above the roar of the common crowd that had gathered to watch the coronation from outside the palace gates, he heard her voice again. Screaming his name desperately. He took a long, haggard breath.

"I must be losing my mind.…" Kareef whispered. "I keep imagining I hear her."

"Who? Jasmine?" Rafiq said. "She's right there."

Kareef whirled sharply. And there, on the other side of the palace gate, surrounded by shoving, cheering crowds, he saw her.

He whirled back to the vizier. "Get her in here!" he thundered.

"Sire," Akmal Al'Sayr begged, "please. She's been trying to get in all night but I've done my best to keep her out. For the good of the country you must consider…"

With a gasp, Kareef grabbed the older man by the neck. Then, with a shuddering breath, he regained control.

"Bring her to me," he ordered between his teeth. Terrified, his vizier gave the frantic order to the guards. A moment later, Jasmine was inside the gate.

She ran straight to his arms. She was dressed in a simple red cotton smock and sandals, her dark hair loose and flying behind her.

"Jasmine," he breathed, holding her against his chest. Half the world's leaders were waiting to see him crowned king, and yet he could not let her go. He pulled her back inside the royal garden, to a private spot behind stone walls.

"It was a lie," she gasped out with a sob. "I said those horrible things because I thought I had to push you away. I don't blame you for the accident. Forgive me," she whispered. "I thought I had no choice."

His eyes fell upon the emerald hanging on a gold chain around her neck. Then he saw her left hand…was bare!

"Did you marry him, Jasmine?" he asked, his heart in his throat.

She shook her head. "No. I couldn't do it. I know we can never be together, Kareef, but I couldn't leave Qusay without telling you the truth. I love you. I always have, and I always will."

With a shuddering intake of breath, Kareef held her against his chest, holding her tight as he closed his eyes, turning his face to the sun. A warm breeze swirled against his white robes, against his skin.

And for the first time since yesterday, he felt himself live again. Felt his blood rushing back through his veins. Felt air fill his lungs with every breath. *Jasmine loved him.*

"You had to know," she whispered. "I had to tell you. I couldn't leave with that lie."

"Leave?" His eyebrows furrowed. "Where are you going?"

"To New York." She gave a small laugh. "To start a new life. My new old life. And it's where," she said softly, "the king of Qusay will always have someone who loves him from afar. I will never forget you. Never stop loving you. Even after you take a wife—"

He stopped her with a kiss. And when he felt her lips against his—her soul against his own, so sweet and strong—he knew what he had to do.

Kareef would honor the vow he'd made long ago. He would hold true to his deepest obligation.

Taking her hand in his own, he led her out of the royal garden. His brother Rafiq was waiting patiently on the other side of the courtyard. Kareef felt a pang, then hardened his heart. It was the right choice. The only choice. Ancient honor demanded it of him, honor deeper than bloodlines. This promise superseded any other.

But still…

Forgive me, he thought, closing his eyes. Then he turned to Jasmine. "Come," he said quietly. "Before you leave this city forever, you will watch me speak the words that bind me."

CHAPTER ELEVEN

As Kareef led her across the courtyard toward the old Byzantine ruin on the edge of the cliff, Jasmine knew it would be painful to watch him speak the words that would make him forever Qusay's king. But she took a deep breath and followed him anyway. She loved him, and knew this would be the last time she would ever see him. She wanted their last memory together to be of her face shining with love—not those horrible words she'd said to him last night.

He abruptly let go of her hand, leaving her behind the three hundred guests seated in chairs placed tightly amid the old stone columns. Kareef and his brother Prince Rafiq continued walking, straight up the aisle of the ancient, roofless ruin.

She felt some people turn to look at her, a few with scorn, others with envy. Then they turned back around as Kareef faced them. He shook hands with his brother before Rafiq bowed and left to sit in the audience beside her old friend Sera. Those two seemed rather cozy, Jasmine thought. Was there something going on between Prince Rafiq and the Sheikha's widowed companion? Then the music swelled, and suddenly no one was looking at Jasmine at all.

Kareef stood at the front in his white ceremonial robes with the jeweled sword at his hip, set in emeralds, and no one could look anywhere else. Tears rose to Jasmine's eyes. He was strength. He was power.

He was her love.

As the vizier started to speak in the old dialect of Qusay, her heart lifted as she stared at Kareef, so regal before the crowd. Even now, after it had ended in heartbreak, Jasmine couldn't regret their affair.

She wouldn't regret loving him—ever.

The music suddenly stopped. She heard the wind, the sound of the waves crashing beneath the cliffs. The ruins of the thousand-year-old citadel seemed to vibrate beneath their feet.

The vizier paused, and as the ceremony demanded, Kareef turned to the crowds. He was darkly beautiful. The perfect king.

His eyes met hers across the audience. And he spoke.

Not in the old dialect, as the ritual decreed, but in words everyone could understand, in a clear, low voice that rang across sand and sea.

"I renounce the throne."

There was a gasp like thunder, echoing across the crowd. She heard the vizier cry out in distress. Someone else gave a low shocked hiss—was it his brother?

Kareef remained steadfast and calm, the eye of the storm.

"Thirteen years ago, I asked a woman to marry me. A young virgin, pure and true." Everyone fell silent, struggling to listen as he said with a harsh lift of his chin and glittering eyes, "That woman was Jasmine Kouri."

A gasp arose from half the crowd as they turned to look at her. "The Kouri girl." The whispers were repeated, even as the foreign dignitaries frowned in bewildered confusion. "The old scandal."

Kareef's face hardened. "Jasmine bore the scandal—alone. But there was no shame. She lost our child in an accident. But before that, she was my bride." He stretched out his arms and proclaimed, "I owe her a debt that supersedes any other duty or obligation."

She was in shock, her heart in her throat as people got whiplash looking between them.

He took a single step down from the dais, his blue eyes locked on hers.

"Jasmine Kouri, you will marry me."

"No," she gasped.

He stepped down to the aisle.

"Jasmine Kouri, you will marry me," he commanded.

She stared at him, unable to answer against the pounding desire of her own heart.

He continued to come down the aisle, his eyes never looking away from hers. Suddenly, he was right in front of her. He towered over her, his body inches from hers. All eyes were upon them.

"Jasmine Kouri," he said softly, "you will marry me."

There was a breathless hush across the ruin.

She looked up at him with tears in her eyes.

"Yes," she choked out, her heart full of joy. "Yes. Yes!"

The smile of happiness across his handsome face

was like nothing she'd ever seen. He took her in his arms and kissed her.

"Now," he whispered urgently when he finally pulled away. "Right now."

"I love you," she whispered in reply.

The vizier rose behind him like a furious serpent. The old man's beard waggled in rage and frustration before he turned away sourly.

"Kareef Al'Ramiz has renounced the throne," the vizier pronounced in a hollow voice that echoed beyond the ancient ruin, across the sea. "There must always be a king of Qusay. Long live…King Rafiq!"

With a gasp, everyone turned to stare at Kareef's brother, the tycoon from Australia. The most shocked of them all appeared to be Rafiq himself. His blue eyes went wide as he looked down at the woman beside him. Jasmine saw Sera's lovely face constrict in shock and pain.

But as all chaos broke around them, her view of Sera and Rafiq was blocked by Kareef's strong, powerful body.

"Say it," he ordered, looking down at her.

"I marry you," she whispered in a voice almost too quiet to hear.

"Louder."

"I marry you."

He looked down at her, his eyes shining with love. "One more time."

And this time, when she spoke, her shout was loud and pure and true. "I marry you!"

He pulled the emerald necklace from her neck and placed it around his throat. Cupping her face in his hands in front of half the world's princes and ambassadors, he gently kissed away the tears now streaking her face.

"And I marry you," he said, completing the ancient Qusani ritual of marriage. As some of the audience burst into applause, and the rest muttered their shock, Kareef took her hand. As she looked up into her husband's handsome, brutal, beloved face, all the storm disappeared around them, blowing away like sand.

"Come, my love," he whispered tenderly. "Let's go home."

Six months later, Jasmine brought her baby out of the house to sit in the morning sun. Cuddling Aziza in her lap in a comfortable, shaded chair, she took a drink of ice water from her own cool glass as she watched her husband train a new yearling in a nearby paddock outside the desert ranch house.

The sun was hot and bright in the blue sky, and around their snug, comfortable home, the horizon stretched out with endless freedom.

But the desert was more than just a horizon. It was more than just sand. If a person looked closer, they'd see so much more, Jasmine thought. Tiny pink flowers. Cactus trees. Hawks soaring through the sky and tiny rabbits darting beneath the rocks. What appeared to be barren was truly full of life and color and joy.

"Jasmine!" When Kareef saw them, he left the other trainers and came over to them. Climbing through the fence, he bent to kiss her, then took the happily gurgling baby in his arms. "Come to teach our daughter how to ride?"

Jasmine choked back a laugh. "She's a bit young yet."

The baby cooed, watching the unbroken horses run in a nearby field. She waved her pudgy arms excitedly. Kareef glanced from his daughter to his wife with a lifted eyebrow.

"All right, it'll happen soon enough," Jasmine said, smiling. "She has your recklessness."

Kneeling before her, he wrapped his arms around them both and looked intently into Jasmine's eyes. "She has your courage."

As he held them both in the strong, protective circle of his arms, the sun was warm on Jasmine's back. She leaned against him as they watched the wild horses running across the field. And Aziza laughed. It was a precious sound, one she never tired of hearing, like the ringing of joyful bells across the desert.

What a precious gift. What a precious life.

Jasmine had set out to give her youngest sister the chance for a fresh start, but Nima had done it for her instead. She'd never wavered on wanting to give her child up for adoption, insisting she was too young and immature to be a decent parent. The day after Jasmine's marriage to Kareef, Nima had called her with a tearful, solemn request. "Take my baby, Jasmine. No one on earth would be a better mother."

It had taken months before Jasmine had finally accepted that Nima wouldn't change her mind. She hadn't really believed it until the day she and Kareef had brought their newborn baby back home.

Nima now lived in New York City, where she attended prep school and next year would start university, with dreams of studying chemistry and biology. She'd visited Qusay several times since the adoption, but she'd made her position clear. "I'm her aunt," Nima had said firmly, then glanced between Jasmine and Kareef with warmth and gratitude shining from her face. "Aziza knows who her real parents are."

Jasmine's parents and sisters already doted on the newest member of the Kouri family, and had visited their home in Qais multiple times. Even her father could not complain—how could he be anything but proud of the daughter who'd snagged a king, pulling him from his throne into a respectable marriage?

Or at least that was her father's gruff excuse, but the truth was that even his iron pride hadn't been able to resist their baby. No one could resist Aziza. Least of all Jasmine.

The happiness of getting everything she'd ever wanted—just when she'd thought all chance was lost—caused her heart to expand so wide in her chest she thought it might break with joy.

Kareef kissed their gurgling baby's chubby cheeks, then moved to kiss his wife's forehead. With a new spark in his eyes, he gave Jasmine a hungry look and lowered his mouth to hers. His kiss was tender and full of passion and promise for the night. When he pulled away, she sighed with happiness.

Each day, he kissed her as if for the first time.

Against all expectation, her life, like the desert, had bloomed. And she knew the heat of the sun, the vast blue sky, and the warmth of their love would last forever.

A wanton widow

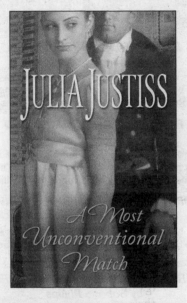

Hal Waterman has secretly adored newly widowed Elizabeth Lowery for years. When he calls upon Elizabeth to offer his help, his silent, protective presence awakens feelings in her that she does not understand.

Elizabeth knows that society would condemn her, but Hal's attractions may well prove too much to resist!

Available 16th April 2010

millsandboon.co.uk Community

Join Us!

The Community is the perfect place to meet and chat to kindred spirits who love books and reading as much as you do, but it's also the place to:

- ■ Get the inside scoop from authors about their latest books
- ■ Learn how to write a romance book with advice from our editors
- ■ Help us to continue publishing the best in women's fiction
- ■ Share your thoughts on the books we publish
- ■ Befriend other users

Forums: Interact with each other as well as authors, editors and a whole host of other users worldwide.

Blogs: Every registered community member has their own blog to tell the world what they're up to and what's on their mind.

Book Challenge: We're aiming to read 5,000 books and have joined forces with The Reading Agency in our inaugural Book Challenge.

Profile Page: Showcase yourself and keep a record of your recent community activity.

Social Networking: We've added buttons at the end of every post to share via digg, Facebook, Google, Yahoo, technorati and de.licio.us.

www.millsandboon.co.uk

2 FREE BOOKS
AND A SURPRISE GIFT

We would like to take this opportunity to thank you for reading this Mills & Boon® book by offering you the chance to take TWO more specially selected books from the Modern™ series absolutely FREE! We're also making this offer to introduce you to the benefits of the Mills & Boon® Book Club™—

- **FREE home delivery**
- **FREE gifts and competitions**
- **FREE monthly Newsletter**
- **Exclusive Mills & Boon Book Club offers**
- **Books available before they're in the shops**

Accepting these FREE books and gift places you under no obligation to buy, you may cancel at any time, even after receiving your free books. Simply complete your details below and return the entire page to the address below. You don't even need a stamp!

YES Please send me 2 free Modern books and a surprise gift. I understand that unless you hear from me, I will receive 4 superb new books every month for just £3.19 each, postage and packing free. I am under no obligation to purchase any books and may cancel my subscription at any time. The free books and gift will be mine to keep in any case.

Ms/Mrs/Miss/Mr _____ Initials _____

Surname _____
Address _____

_____ Postcode _____
E-mail _____

Send this whole page to: Mills & Boon Book Club, Free Book Offer, FREEPOST NAT 10298, Richmond, TW9 1BR

First published in Great Britain 2012
by Mills & Boon, an imprint of Harlequin (UK) Limited,
Eton House, 18-24 Paradise Road, Richmond, Surrey TW9 1SR

© Pamela Palmer Poulsen 2012

ISBN: 978 0 263 89605 3
ebook ISBN: 978 1 408 97488 9

089-0712

Harlequin (UK) policy is to use papers that are natural, renewable and recyclable products and made from wood grown in sustainable forests. The logging and manufacturing processes conform to the legal environmental regulations of the country of origin.

Printed and bound in Spain
by Blackprint CPI, Barcelona

WARRIOR RISING

PAMELA PALMER

MILLS &
BOON